# never yours

## irene bahrd

*For Elizabeth… and her ~~fake ass~~ fictional brother.*

# content warnings & author note

By reading this book, there is a good chance you will experience the following side effects:

- Wet panties
- Looking into which of your friends has a hot, single brother
- Renting a boat, just so you can fuck someone on it
- Adopting a Dalmatian

*You're welcome.*

All jokes aside, this is a slow(ish)-burn, low-to-medium spice, romantic comedy that still has a healthy dose of on-page explicit content. It is intended for mature audiences. Because it's lower spice than my other books, expect to only break out your buzzbuzz a few times before it's over.

While this is technically a romantic comedy, there are some scenes and topics that may be uncomfortable for some readers. Others will treat this as a shopping list:

- Oral sexytime — it's an Irene Bahrd trademark, you knew it was coming
- Brief scene with cockwarming... sort of. More of a cockwarming gone wrong
- A bunch of vanilla sex — sorry
- Mild bondage — he just ties her up a little for a minute
- Butt stuff in the epilogue

Okay, we've had our fun. Now for the real content warnings...

- Dubious consent (not with Caleb)
- Off-page miscarriage (happened in the past)
- Off-page death of a doggo (not the Caleb or Ingrid's)
- Accidental pregnancy
- Discussions about abortion and access to women's healthcare
- Brief discussion of the broken health care system (specifically the military)
- Off-page cesarean
- On-page military deployment
- On-page PTSD (Caleb)

If you are triggered by anything in this book, do us both a favor and don't read anything else in my backlist, the rest of my books are equally unhinged. But, to be fair, my other books won't be this emotional.

**Author Note:** This is <u>NOT</u> a how-to guide. You will probably be arrested if caught fucking on a boat. Also, condoms are only used once in this book. Please be safe and talk to your doctor about what works best for you and/or your sexual partners regarding pregnancy and STIs. Ingrid and Caleb are fictional, you are not.

Additionally, sensitivity readers were consulted in the portrayal of Caleb and his on-page PTSD. The events in this book are **completely fictional,** not based off real life events. No ship was hit in the Pacific... that I know of. However, the scenes with Caleb having an anxiety attack and/or experiencing PTSD were based off the suggestion from two military officers who have had similar experiences. They reviewed the scenes, and though this work of fiction accurately portrays anxiety or PTSD for *those* service members, anxiety, depression, and PTSD are unique to every individual. My hope is that this book shines light on the struggles that some service members have.

# playlist

I Don't Care — Ed Sheeran [feat. Justin Bieber]
Not Over You — Gavin Degraw
Delicate — Taylor Swift
Just Give Me a Reason — P!nk [feat. Nate Ruess]
She will Be Loved — Maroon 5
You Were Meant For Me — Jewel
Shadow — Lady Gaga [feat. Bradley Cooper]
Beautiful Things — Benson Boone
Beautiful Day — U2

# prologue

. . .

Caleb

**Please read Content Warnings & Author Note prior to reading.**

I fucking hate prom.

You rent a tux that would blind you under UV lights, show up at your date's house to be berated by her father, take her to dinner—*your parents paying for said dinner*—and you wind up at a sweaty gym or banquet hall, grinding your cock against a girl you invited out of pity... because you were too chicken shit to ask the one girl you wanted to take.

*Fucking. Joke.*

As predicted, my date, Lindsay, is dancing with her friends, leaving me to sulk in the corner; like Pop did in his emo phase. I don't dance, so it's a blessing in disguise. At least eight girls have tried to drag me over for a glorified dry hump, but my answer remains no.

Through it all, I can't take my eyes off Ingrid. She's huddled on the other side of the room, reading a fantasy book I finished last year, leaving me with two options:

1. Approach with caution, and word-vomit every detail I can remember from the book.
2. Become a fucking statue and allow paralysis to overcome me.

Both options end in failure, leaving me to admire her from my standard-issue, plastic chair.

"Hey, fuckface," Travis teases, pulling my attention from Ingrid.

Without skipping a beat, I ask with a cocked eyebrow, "Where's Tara?"

"Probably recovering from me fucking her in the locker room shower." Travis shrugs as I cough a laugh. "What? She was begging for it!" When I don't respond, he asks, "When are you going to ask her?"

"Who?" I follow his line of sight, falling on Ingrid. With a deep sigh, I insist, "It's not like that. She's my sister's friend." She isn't just Cassidy's best friend, she's mine, too; the one person who gets me.

Being only eleven months younger than my sister, we've been in the same grade throughout school. I'd never date one of her friends—if it didn't work out, my relationship with Cass would never be the same. We found out the hard way when she dated one of mine two years ago.

Ingrid is different. It wouldn't just ruin my friendship with Ingrid, it would destroy Cassidy.

"Fuck that," he laughs. "It's about time you were devirginized."

"What?" I sputter.

"Get your dick wet. You're shipping out in a month, you don't want to leave with your V-card." Travis glances over his shoulder and chuckles, spotting Tara giving him a come-hither glare. "Looks like she's ready for round two."

I roll my eyes as he rushes in her direction. He's already packed and ready to leave for the fire academy a few towns over and is determined to get laid as much as possible before he leaves. I suppose I should consider one night of no-strings-attached, too… if I could manage to tear my eyes away from Ingrid. With my luck, I'd call out the wrong name with someone else as I come. I don't want anyone else, I want *her*.

Ingrid's off-limits, and we'll never be more than friends, but what if this is my shot, my one chance to be with her?

About to make my way to Ingrid and risk everything, I only take three steps before I stop in my tracks. She stands, clapping her book together and stuffing it into her tote— which doesn't match her dress.

"Asshole," I'm able to make out from lip-reading.

I glance to the dance floor that's holding her attention and find her date lip-locked with… *Lindsay?* Why Ingrid said 'yes' to the captain of the varsity football team in the first place is beyond me; they have nothing in common. Then again, I have nothing in common with Lindsay and asked her. Taking all of two seconds to contemplate it, I continue to walk over to Ingrid. She doesn't appear to need consoling, but I've always been there for her—her person. Just as she's always been mine.

When I reach Ingrid, she greets me with a hug as she always does, and I kiss her temple. Our embrace is longer than usual, but neither one of us lets go.

"I'm sorry about those two," she sighs against me. "I want to get out of—"

I don't care that we're just friends. I don't care if my date used me to come to prom. I don't care that Ingrid might use me, too. I grip her chin between my thumb and forefinger and kiss her. For the briefest of moments, she melts into me. Just as quickly, her eyes fly wide, and she steps out of my hold.

"Cay, we can't."

"Why not?" She stills in my arms. "I don't want to sleep with you." The lie weighs on me, but I would be more than happy to spend the rest of the night with her fully clothed.

"Then, what do you want?" Her brows pinch.

*You.*

Unable to admit it, I deflect, "What do *you* want?"

Ingrid's expression softens. "Can we get out of here?"

Without another word, I take her hand and rush us out of the gym and to my pop's truck. She doesn't pull away, and I hang onto the tiny glimmer of hope that she feels the same way about me that I do about her. "Where to, princess?"

"Princess?" she laughs. "You know better than anyone that I'm hardly a princess."

"Could've fooled me with that tiara." I open the door and gesture for her to get in. "Your chariot awaits."

She smiles, biting her lip, teasing, "And they say chivalry is dead." Reaching up, she removes the tiara and tosses it haphazardly into the cab of the truck.

Offering my hand to help her get in, she doesn't take it. It's always been this way with her; never needing anyone. I close the door and round the pick-up to get in on the driver's side. The moment I'm next to her, I'm met with her floral perfume, reminding me of when we used to sit on her porch reading. Daffodils. Just like the ones that her mother grows every spring right next to the porch.

We drive down the quiet road, and the silence is deafening. As I'm about to ask her about the book she was reading, she breaks it first and quietly asks, "Why did you take Lindsay?"

"The person I wanted to go with was already going with someone else." I fail to hide my smile, except she doesn't return it.

Keeping my eyes on the road. I still manage to see her quickly look away and out of the window. Her voice small, she mutters, "It's not like you would've asked me." *What the fuck?* I pull over to the side of the road. "What are you doing?"

Putting the truck into 'park,' I turn and face her. "I wanted to ask you, but you already had a date."

Her eyes lock with mine, leaving me wondering how badly I'll fuck things up with Cass if I consider this. My eyes fall to Ingrid's dark red lips, her chest rising and falling with erratic breaths, when she surprises me, taking my face in her hands and kissing me. Her lips are soft and warm, making me forget every reason I have for not being with her.

Ingrid pulls back an inch, rests her forehead on mine, and whispers, "If you had asked, I would've said yes."

# ingrid

. . .

Ten Years Later

"**F**uck, you feel so good."

*What the hell am I supposed to say to that? Thanks?*

Sleeping with my boss has to be the worst decision I've ever made; there's no way I'm going to be able to show my face at work tomorrow. But, when the head of your network comes onto you, you're left with two options: give in and quit, or reject him and risk being fired. Quitting is easier than getting fired. With the gossip around the office, it was only a matter of time before this asshole came onto me—I should've worn a wedding ring to work or insisted I'm only into women. Then again, that didn't stop him from ruining Denise Kensington's career. She "quit" shortly after a meeting alone with him a few months back.

I've spent the last five years working my ass off to become a head writer for *Left Field*—the network's number one sitcom. All to have the rug pulled out from under me.

*"Meet me in my office to discuss the new show idea you're proposing," he said. "I'll clear my calendar."*

Bull. Fucking. Shit.

The cold leather couch bounces beneath me as Martin thrusts faster, guaranteeing I'll be putting on a performance. I give it two minutes before I have to moan his name. It doesn't help that 'Martin' isn't the sexiest to call out—more like I'll be summoning a butler. My best option is to completely dissociate and pretend this is just a bad sex dream.

*If I wanted a bad sex dream, I would just go through the highlight reel of prom night, when I lost one of my best friends after sleeping with him.*

Martin tenses up and, after no more than sixty seconds, he pants my name and fills the condom. *Shit, I missed my cue.* "Martin," I grit out as I clench my pussy around his unimpressive thin cock. I keep up with my kegels, but this is a hotdog down a hallway situation here. I can only do so much.

"That's right. Milk my cock."

*What the fuck? It's hot in books. This guy? Hard pass.*

"Mr. Harris? You have John Grant on line three," Alicia announces through the phone intercom on his desk.

*Fuck, I hope she didn't hear all that.*

Martin pulls out of me and replies back to her, "Let him know I'm finishing up a meeting," then lowers his voice and tells me, "As soon as I'm done with this call, I want you on your knees with those pouty red lips wrapped around my cock."

Bile rises in my throat, but I manage to paint on a sweet smile. "Can't stay. I have an episode to write."

There's no episode to write. This season is over, and I have already handed my notes to the producers for next season. I've gathered enough from our "meeting" that he doesn't keep track of the sitcom schedules, so my lie should survive.

"Tomorrow, then."

I nod, and he lifts off me, pulling off the condom and tying it. Swiftly shifting my panties back in place that he carelessly moved to the side, I inwardly chastise myself for letting this happen. My pussy may not be ruined, but my career most definitely is.

As I'm about to leave, he leans in to kiss me, and I instinctively slap him. Slapped my fucking boss. So much for quitting, I'll probably be fired with assault charges pressed against me.

"You like it rough?" he laughs, rubbing his cheek.

He's not wrong, but I wouldn't let him touch me again if my life depended on it. Scurrying out of the office, he laughs, unfazed by it all. I pass Alicia's desk, and she pins me with a knowing glare. She's the office gossip with too much fucking time on her hands. Within the next hour, everyone will know what I've done, sealing my unemployed fate as the woman who unsuccessfully screwed her way to the top—even if it's all lies.

I was fucked if I did and fucked if I didn't. I should have said no, but no other network would pick me up if I was fired. Now? That slap may have cost me more than being head writer, I may never write for primetime television again.

I need to get away.

As I walk to my desk, I type out a text to Cassidy.

Can I stay with you for a bit?

CASSIDY
Big city finally get to you?

Fucked my boss.

Shit.

And slapped him.

Ok, but that's hot.

It really wasn't.

Dad has a house for rent that's been sitting for a bit. Consider it yours as long as you need it.

Did you even ask him?

No, but you know he'll say yes.

I can't help but chuckle. Even though I haven't been back home since high school, she's right, he'll insist I stay there; I still get Christmas cards every year.

Hope the sex was good, at least.

Worst of my life.

I don't add that it was the worst other than sleeping with her brother. It wasn't Caleb's fault, he didn't know I was a virgin. I faked it then, and I've faked it ever since. Sex just isn't for me, I'm always better off with my toys.

> Fuck, that sucks.

> Just let me know when you're coming.

> To Sapphire Lake. I don't need to know when you're mid-orgasm.

> Are you sure? I can send you video evidence of my self care.

> If you insist. But know that I'll be posting it online. It has to do better than my feet pics. Have to pay my student loans somehow!

Discreetly packing up my desk, I reply that I'm going to grab a flight out of New York tomorrow. I refuse to stay here a minute longer than absolutely necessary. I need her, I need home. Hell, I even need Caleb at this point. We used to be so close; I don't remember the last time I had someone in my life who cared about me the way Cassidy's family does.

I practically sprint out of the office with my belongings; my resignation letter will need to wait. Thankfully, no one stops me, but when I make it out to the street, my tears finally fall and blend with the dewy mist falling from the sky. I've lost everything in the space of one afternoon. For a brief moment, I let my emotions get the best of me and allow myself to cry for the first time in a decade.

*Stop it! You're Ingrid Fucking Lawrence. This will not break you.*

With a deep breath I will my tears back and hail a cab, leaving behind the career I built.

But I'm taking my pride with me.

# caleb

. . .

"**C**an you get the Rose Road property ready for me today?" Pop says into his pint.

Setting down the glass I'm drying, I excitedly ask, "It's finally rented?" It's been sitting empty forever, and he could use the extra income.

"Sort of," he mutters, taking a long drink of his beer, avoiding the question he knows is coming. My cocked eyebrow is enough and he says simply, "It's Ingrid."

"In—" My stomach drops, and I swallow hard. "Ingrid Lawrence?"

A small smirk tugs at his lips. "Maybe."

"She's visiting Cass?"

"Something like that." He takes another drink, trying to hide his amused smile. Carefully resting his now-empty pint on the bar, he adds, "Need the property done by tonight."

"Tonight?" I choke, then glance over at the large wall clock. "I don't get off for another four hours."

"Shit, she's supposed to be in town in two. I'll see if Mike can do it." Pop takes out his phone and reading glasses. He's only forty-eight, but I swear he acts like he's ninety sometimes, especially when it comes to technology. Explaining what a meme is to him gave Cass a good laugh. "How do you send a GIF?"

*There it is.*

"Give it here." I offer my hand, and he passes me the phone. "What one do you want?"

"Is there a pussy-whipped cartoon character with heart eyes?"

I slide the phone across the bar and laugh, "You're on your own. That ship has sailed." That ship has *not* sailed, no one has ever held a candle to her.

He joins in on my laughter, but his face falls at the mention of 'ship.' "You just got back, Cay." He shuts his eyes tightly and takes a deep breath. When he opens them, his voice is strangled when he asks, "Last one?"

"Last one," I assure him. "I'll be back before you know it."

As I resume hand-drying glasses, he types on his phone, then stuffs it into his back pocket. "She'll be coming by the bar, could you give her a ride to the house?"

"What?" I cough. The bar is suddenly too small.

"Keep it in your pants, son. I don't know the details, but" —he rakes his hand through his salt-and-pepper hair—

"Cass said Ingrid's going through some shit; might be here for a while. Give her time, okay?"

*So help me, if someone hurt her…*

My jaw tightens, and a growl inadvertently rumbles from my chest, but I'm startled by a clap on the back. "Down, tiger," Cassidy laughs.

"Fuck, Cass, you scared the shit outta me."

"Language," Pop snaps. "Watch your fucking mouth." Cass and I laugh while he slides off his seat. "Well, I'm going to check on the house."

"What about Mike?" I ask with a frown. Pop shouldn't be doing it by himself. The house has been sitting for a while, and anything could be wrong with it at this point.

"He's busy with his kid. Karate or something." He shrugs and asks Cassidy, "Can you come by with flowers for Ingrid? Are daffodils still her favorite?"

*How the fuck does he know that?*

"Yeah, I'll stop by Dani's shop and have her put something together." Joining Pop on the other side of the bar, she adds, "If he forgot to tell you, Ingrid's coming by the bar later. Please give her a ride since I have to work… Don't get any ideas."

"What the hell? First Pop, now you?"

She chuckles and wraps an arm around Pop. "I'll come see her on my lunch break." Her levity ceases, and she chews on her lip. "Just… don't. Please. We all know you had a crush on her in high school…"

Pop huffs a laugh. "That's putting it lightly."

"Out, both of you," I groan, even though he's right. Neither of them know what happened on prom night, and I intend to keep it that way, but it pisses me off that Ingrid's hurting enough that she's back home.

It must be written all over my face when Pop sighs, "You're a good man, son. But listen to your sister, for once."

With a nod, they both walk out of the bar, leaving me to finish getting everything ready for the after-work rush. My mind is reeling after talking with them, wondering what the hell is going on with Ingrid.

Two hours, three kegs replaced, and both ice bins filled later, I have nothing to do until the only woman I've ever loved is supposed to show up. If I'm being honest, I don't know if it was truly love, or just a teenage obsession, but either way, I'll be heeding my family's warning until I find out what brought her back home.

*Who am I kidding? All it would take is seeing her beautiful smile again I'd be a fucking goner—like I'm still in fucking high school.*

Another thirty minutes pass, and I'm kicking myself for not asking when she would be stopping by. Pop said two hours until she was in town, but depending on if she is visiting with friends first, it could be ten minutes or another hour. The anticipation is killing me.

Lauren puts on her half apron and steps behind the bar with a wide smile. As she finishes tying it, she leans against the counter. "So… anything *exciting* happening today?"

"Nope," I lie, untying my own apron. "Going to take ten before the rush."

"Wouldn't have anything to do with Ingrid being back in town, would it?" She wiggles her eyebrows. "I get it. I follow her on social media, she's fucking hot." I stifle a groan, and as I'm about to storm off, she grips my wrist. "I'm kidding! Well, not really, she *is* hot. But, I ran into your dad at the hardware store earlier, and he mentioned fixing a sink for her."

"What's wrong with the sink?" Unfortunately, it comes out like a fucking growl, making Lauren laugh.

"Relax! It's fine. Sheesh, you're on edge. It's just a small leak so he's replacing the faucet." She smirks, entirely too excited about this. In the last year that we've worked together, she's seen me go on exactly two dates, merely to placate the nosy people in town. Meanwhile, she's fucked nearly all of the men here, and half the women—or at least it feels that way. Even though it was a decade ago, I'm still hung up on the girl who got away. "Take your break. Your dad said she's coming by, so I'll let you know the moment she comes in."

Lauren playfully shoves me a few feet toward the door, and I walk the rest of the way out back to sweep the patio. With the sky gray and more clouds rolling in, it's unlikely anyone will be out here tonight, but with my stomach in knots, I need to keep busy to quiet my mind.

Misted raindrops dust my hair, so once the patio is cleared off, I head back inside. Just like the night that ruined me, I only make it three steps before I pause, rooted in place. My stomach drops, and my heart leaps out of my damn chest. I can't fucking breathe.

*Ingrid.*

All at once, memories of the best and worst night of my life hit me. But seeing Ingrid after all this time feels like a piece of a puzzle I've been searching for. *She's here.* Lauren is laughing with Tim at the end of the bar. Spotting me, she mouths "sorry" but continues talking to him. I don't blame her, Tim always tips her well.

Ingrid's laughing with Travis who's sitting to her right. Approaching with caution, I put my apron back on and blow out a long breath—now is as good a time as any to make a fucking fool of myself. Spotting an ereader face-down on the bar, I interrupt them.

"What'cha reading?"

*What'cha reading? That's the best you've got? I'm already screwing this up.*

Ingrid and Travis stop talking and look at me. She glances between us a few times, then sheepishly replies, "Oh, hi. Um, it's... *fiction.*" Though I'm sure it's smut, she won't admit it in front of Travis.

"Fiction?"

"Yup. Just good, old-fashioned fiction," she insists a little too quickly, her cheeks dusted a light pink.

Travis rests his arm on the back of her chair. "Can we get another round?" He lifts his shot glass, but my eyes don't move from where he is dangerously close to what's mine.

My jaw tics. "Sure. What are you drinking?"

"Tequila, please," she answers for them.

*Fuck, is she on a date with him?*

I pour a double shot of reposado, sliding it to her, then pour a second for Travis. "Bad week?"

Ingrid groans, "The worst."

Travis attempts to pay me, but I shake my head. "On me."

Her eyes rake my body, and even though I enjoy her checking me out, I can't help feeling a pang of hurt that she doesn't recognize me. Granted, we haven't spoken since that night, and I'm a good thirty pounds of muscle heavier with a beard I've been growing since I got home, but it still stings.

It also doesn't excuse Travis for taking her out the first night she's in town; he knows what she means to me. Pop didn't give me much to go on, but I sure as hell hope he's not the reason she's back after all these years.

Feeling my blood pressure rise, I move down the bar and pour beer for a few of my regulars. Even with her being on a date, Ingrid's paying more attention to what I'm doing than whatever Travis is saying to her. I do my best to hide my enjoyment of her brushing off his advances, but satisfaction gets the best of me, and I can't help smiling and stealing glances of her.

After ten minutes, Travis appears to give up and puts cash down on the bar. *That's right. Back off. She's mine.* Sliding off his seat, he puts on his SLFD cap and shouts to me with a smirk, "See you next week, Rogers."

I nod, and he leaves, allowing me to focus my attention back on my favorite redhead. As I am pouring her another shot, she searches my eyes for a moment before hers widen.

*"Cay?"*

# ingrid

. . .

"**S**ee you next week, Rogers," Travis shouts to our bartender as he leaves the bar.

*Rogers?*

*No. No, no, no.*

*He's taller, filled out, and… a beard?*

*Fuck, he looks good.*

*No. It can't be Cay. Can it?*

*It has to be his cousin.*

*Cass and Caleb don't have cousins…*

"Cay?" I squeak, praying I'm wrong and it didn't look like I was flirting with Travis in front of him. The moment his boyish grin paints his face, the air whooshes from my lungs. I down the shot and quickly place a slice of lime between my teeth.

"Another?"

"Uh-huh," I reply, my voice an octave higher and shaky, and he pours one more.

Fucking Cassidy. She said she'd have "someone" drive me home from the bar; she didn't mention it could be Caleb. When I saw Travis, I thought for sure it was him, until he said he was about to start a seventy-two-hour shift at the station.

I've successfully avoided Cay for a decade, blocking his profiles on social media so I wouldn't have to be broken-hearted by a possible engagement announcement, wedding photos... Or worse, puppy thirst traps while wearing delicious gray sweatpants. I don't blame him for anything that happened, but I certainly don't want to relive how our friendship ended or how it went down after I left. Especially after this week.

I finish the shot, and as he is about to pour me another double, I shake my head. "I can't. I'll get drunk. When I get drunk, I do the talking thing. We don't need to do the talking thing. No good can come of—" He takes the shot for me, no chaser. "Thank you."

"Go have a seat in one of the booths, finish reading about a chick getting railed, and I'll drive you home when I'm off."

"You're driving me home? I... *Wait.*" My eyes narrow. "I'm not reading about a chick getting railed." Before I can continue, he snatches my ereader from across the bar. "Hey!"

He scrolls for entirely too long as I try to swipe it from him, unsuccessfully. "You're right. Your *fiction* has three men. That's a lot of dick, Ingrid."

"The woman comes in later," I indigently groan, and he cocks an eyebrow as he passes the device back to me. "I mean, I don't know what you're talking about." He's about to take it from me again, so I admit, "Fine! Yes, it's a 'why choose.'" He stares blankly at me. "I'm *not* going to explain it. I've had a shitty week and wanted to read some plotless sm— *fiction* when I ran into Travis."

Caleb laughs, but it's a deep rumble that makes my thighs clench. I shouldn't feel this pull to him after all these years, yet... here we are. He points to the booth in the back of the bar. "Enjoy your plotless fiction. I'm off in a bit, and Pop should have your place fixed up by then."

I reach for the shot glass, lifting it with a small shake. "Well, if it's going to be a while, maybe one more?" He pours me a half shot, and I deadpan, "Really?"

He shrugs. "You said you didn't want to do the 'talking thing.'"

"I changed my mind."

"You don't need it," he growls, and my breath hitches.

"And what is it that I need?" A flicker of fire dances in his eyes. I know I walked into that one, so I dare, "I'm a paying patron, Cay. One *full* shot."

He looks over to the woman at the end of the bar. "Lo! Her money is no good here, and she's eighty-sixed."

"What the fuck?" I screech, drawing attention to us. I repeat in a whisper, "What the fuck?" He rounds the bar until he's towering over me, and fear creeps in—he's fucking massive. As if he can sense it, he takes a seat on the stool next to me, making my heart slow down.

"Trust me," he says softly. "You don't need another drink. Tequila won't fix whatever brought you back home."

"I know," I sigh. I can't look away from his sparkling honey-brown eyes. I'm lost in them… *or maybe the tequila is.*

Caleb tucks my hair behind my ear. I don't flinch like I thought I would as he keeps his fingers cupped behind my neck, his thumb resting on my cheek. "You're home."

"I am." *He* is home. Maybe this is fate?

*No, I've been reading too much plotless smut.*

"It's slow, Cay!" the woman calls to him, making him pull back from me. "I'll close up."

"Thanks," he replies to her, though his eyes never leave mine. Then, he tells me, "Your place isn't ready yet. Want to stay here?"

"Honestly, I'm exhausted. I think I'll take you up on the booth offer and crash for a bit."

"I'll do you one better." He stands and kisses my temple. My heart skips a beat at the small gesture he used to do. After all this time, his touch still grounds me. "You can stay with me tonight. I'll take the couch."

Caleb doesn't let me protest as he takes off his apron and grabs his keys. I slip off my stool, and his hand slides into mine, interlacing our fingers. Leading me out of the bar, I try to take my rolling suitcase, but he insists on doing it himself. As much as I shouldn't, I let him help me.

A few people whisper to each other at the bar, making me nervous. I've never asked Cassidy about Cay; he could be married and just a good friend driving me home. Holding his hand probably makes me look like a homewrecker, so I quickly glance down at our inter-locked fingers to check for obvious signs of matrimony... no ring.

*Maybe divorced?*

The idea that Caleb could be single is both enticing and depressing. Even if I've spent my twenties in loveless rela-tionships, it doesn't mean I wanted that for him.

We make it to his pick-up, and he places the suitcase in the truck bed. As he opens the door, flashbacks flood me from that night—pulling over the side of the road and losing my virginity to one of my best friends.

"Cay, I can't stay with you," I rush out.

There's a brief pause before his reply. "I don't know why you're here, but honestly, I don't care. You don't have to tell me what happened. Just... let me try to make things a little easier for you?" Cay opens the truck door wider. When I don't get in, he lifts me onto the seat like I weigh nothing, then braces himself on the roof of the car. "We can go to your new place and wait a few hours until repairs are done. Or you can rest at my place. What'll it be, princess?"

"You don't need to stay or babysit me. I'll be fine." I sigh. "I was *awful* to you. After losing my vir— *I mean,* after we... *you know.*"

He frowns, and I swear there's a rumble coming from his chest. "What did you just say?"

*Shit. Nothing gets past him.*

"That I was awful to you?"

"No. What did you just say?" His eyes are dark, but I don't know what to make of it other than he probably won't let this go.

"Please don't make me say it," I groan.

"Were you a virgin back when…?"

"What? *Pfft*. No." I keep my expression neutral, but my heart stops. "What does it matter?"

"Because I was. I was young, and a fucking idiot, but *never* for one moment have I regretted it was you."

My mask slips and my heart restarts for the first time in what feels like forever. *It wasn't just me…* With a voice quiet, I finally admit, "I was, too, and I don't regret it was you, either."

"Fuck." Caleb huffs a laugh and slides my legs into the truck, muttering, "The best and worst night of my life."

# caleb

. . .

A s I get into the driver's side and start the truck, Ingrid asks, "It was the worst night of your life?"

Needing to touch her, I take her hand and brush my thumb back-and-forth on hers. "I wanted you for years, and wasted my one shot at being with you."

"We were kids. It never would've gone anywhere. You enlisted and were shipping off in a month; I was leaving for college." She takes a deep breath, but then chuckles softly. "The sex was bad, but I mean it when I say I don't regret you being my first." I close my eyes, and my head hits the headrest. I was so embarrassed when I came way too fast. I still am. "Hey." She cups my cheek, forcing me to look at her, and sighs, "I'm just sorry we couldn't stay friends after."

"Friends. Right." The word stabs me straight in the heart. "We really don't need to talk about this. I shouldn't have said anything." She pulls away and nods, sitting back in her seat as I shift the truck into reverse.

On the road, the silence is eating at me. It was never like this with her, and I fucking hate it. Each street light, every stop sign, the occasional crosswalk with pedestrians—not once does she look forward or at me. She was trying to make light of everything, maybe even a damn olive branch, and I managed to screw it up with my pride.

When we pull up to the house, we remain in our seats, the tension so thick you'd need a fucking chainsaw to cut it. We speak over each other saying, "I'm sorry."

"No," I groan, raking my hand through my hair. "This is on me. I've been on edge since Pop told me you were coming. And then I saw you with Travis…"

Ingrid finally looks at me. "It's not like that with him. We were talking about Cass and… you." Gripping the steering wheel tightly, a growl rattles in my throat. "Cay, what's going on?"

"It was supposed to be you and me," I admit a little too quickly.

Her gaze falls to her hands, fidgeting with the hem of her shirt, shaking her head. "That's sweet. But, we were never together. We hooked up once, ten years ago."

Before I can defend myself, Pop emerges from the house, and I roll down her window as he approaches the truck.

"Hey, Ingrid," he greets cheerfully. "Hope you had a good flight."

Her tone light, she replies, "I did, thank you. And thanks for letting me stay here."

"None of that." Pop waves his hand dismissively. "You're family. I fixed the leaky kitchen faucet, but if you need anything else, you can give me or Caleb a call."

Ingrid nods thoughtfully, and Pop opens the door for her. "Thanks for the ride. I'll… see you around?"

"Yeah, sure." I try to mask my disappointment, but by the look on Pop's face, it may as well be written in marker on my forehead.

Pop grabs her suitcase from the back and walks her to the door. When they reach it, he hands Ingrid a key and says something that has her wrapping her arms tightly around him. Irrational jealousy with a dash of anger—directed at myself—overtakes me, as I white-knuckle the wheel.

Once she's inside, Pop comes back to the truck and places a small tool kit in the front seat. "I gave her your number, but I'm not giving you hers. I told you to keep it in your pants, son." There isn't a hint of teasing in his voice. Cass and Pop warned me Ingrid is going through something, and here I am making things worse by rehashing the past with her.

"Nothing happened," I insist, though I selfishly wish something had.

"Keep it that way," he snaps back, and I honestly don't remember the last time he spoke to me like this. "You're leaving soon."

He's right. I raise my hands in surrender, though I'm sure his worry comes more from my departure than her arrival. "Ok, message received."

His tone softens as he asks, "See you Sunday for brunch?"

"Always."

He claps the truck twice and walks to his parked in the driveway. I drive to the store to pick up a few things, then head home, my mind reeling from today. When I pull up to the house, my phone's home screen shows missed texts and I click on them.

UNKNOWN

I'm sorry about tonight. A lot happened this week that I'm not ready to talk about.

This is Ingrid, by the way.

I chuckle at the qualifier and don't reply back. Instead, I call and she picks up on the first ring. "Cay?"

"Hey."

"Hey."

There's silence for a few moments, until I finally assure her, "There's nothing to apologize for."

"I feel like we should talk about things, but I'm not in the right headspace for it."

"It's ok, we can talk about whatever you want, unless you need more tequila for the 'talking thing.'"

She laughs, making me feel lighter than I have since she got back. "What are you doing right now?"

"I'm sitting outside my house in the truck."

"When you get inside, would you... I'm sorry, this is stupid, but would you mind staying on the phone with me for a bit? Like we used to?"

I huff a small laugh. "Sure. And it's not stupid. Is everything ok?"

"No," she sighs. "It's not."

Hope blooms in my chest that I haven't screwed things up completely if she still wants me to be her person. "I'm here for as long as you need me to be."

# ingrid

. . .

I wake up to the sound of light snoring through the phone; Caleb and I must have fallen asleep last night and never hung up. I don't want to lead him on, but Cass was only here for her lunch break before working the rest of her overnight shift. Being in this empty house, I needed to feel less alone after this shitty week.

Carefully hanging up, I slide out of bed, and pad off to the bathroom, only managing to brush my teeth and pee before my phone begins chiming with news alerts. It must be six thirty—when my phone shifts from sleep to work mode. I should probably change that setting, seeing as I'm unemployed. With a groan, I return to the bedroom to check my phone, finding seventy news articles with my name highlighted. My stomach drops. Nearly every one of them is about me leaving the show and the network.

*Ingrid Lawrence, Head Writer, Leaves Left Field.*

*Left Field Writer, Ingrid Lawrence, Pregnant with Martin Harris' Love Child.*

*Ingrid Lawrence Leaves Left Field for Mystery Man in Sapphire Lake.*

I feel like I'm scrolling endlessly through lie after lie. There's several with speculation that I was fired, and even a few suggest that I'm in rehab. The one that sticks out the most is a candid shot of Caleb sitting next to me at the bar. The way he's looking at me... *No.* I can't entertain the idea that he'd want to be with me after the truth comes out. It's best to keep my distance.

*Lesson learned: There are assholes here in Sapphire Lake who will sell a picture for a buck.*

I'm just glad they didn't get one of me talking to Travis to add fuel to the fire.

I toss my phone onto the nightstand and drag my suitcase across the room, slinging it on the bed. As I unzip it, my clothes fly out like a jack-in-the-box.

"Fuck," I groan and attempt to scoop the contents back into the luggage.

"Coffee?" Cass's question makes me jump. "Or... no coffee?"

"Fuck, where did you come from?" I laugh, gripping my chest.

"You left the door unlocked and didn't answer when I knocked." She sets down both to-go cups on the vanity and wraps me in a tight hug, her scrubs wafting off a strong medicinal scent. "How did you sleep?"

I pat her on the shoulder when she doesn't let go. "Um, good."

"Sorry, just missed you."

"I saw you last night." I roll my eyes and laugh. "But I didn't get to thank you for the heads up that Cay would be driving me home…"

"Oops," she teases, rocking back on her heels.

"Yeah, *oops*." I pull out a pair of black leggings and an oversized tee that's cut so I can wear it off one of my shoulders. "How the hell are you so chipper after an overnight shift?"

"I'm highly caffeinated and have to open up the bar in a few hours before Cay or Lo take over." She shrugs and grabs her coffee, gulping half of it.

"Fuck, I'm too old for that shit. Give me an early night with a lavender bath bomb any day."

I'm about to get changed, when Cass stops me. "So…" She chews on her lip. "You know you can stay here as long as you'd like, but have you made any plans? Are you going to write remotely?" She lowers her voice and jests, "Going to rehab?"

"You saw that?" I cringe. "No rehab for me." I don't know what I want to do yet, but I already feel better being back home. I undress in front of her and slip on my clean clothes. It doesn't phase her, even though she hasn't seen me naked since high school gym class.

Grabbing my coffee, I take a sip, nearly spitting it out when she asks, "Caleb didn't stay the night. So, you're not going to be my future sister-in-law?"

"Hardly." I wipe my mouth as I sputter a cough. "We talked a little, but that's it."

"Bummer," she teases, taking an exaggerated long drink of her coffee.

"I'm not in a good place to date right now, *especially* someone like your brother."

Cass playfully narrows her eyes at me. "Hey, what's wrong with my brother?"

*Nothing, he's fucking perfect.*

"He's *your* brother," I sigh. "And I'm the disgraced sitcom writer who fled New York. I'd break his heart, like I did all those years ago after we slept—"

My hand flies to my mouth, and before I can retract it, she gasps, "You fucked Cay, didn't you?"

"Nope." I shake my head, but she's not buying what I'm selling. Her eyes narrow, and I concede, "Ok, fine, yes. We slept together. *Once…* Prom night." Not an ounce of shock paints her face, her eyes are instead alight with mischief. I rush out, "But that's it, nothing else happened! I was a bitch, ignoring him, and then he went off to the Navy, and I went off to college, and we never spoke again, and—" A wide grin appears, and I glare at her. "You knew."

"Don't worry, he didn't tell me, but I always assumed something happened when you two left together. Why didn't you tell me?" She continues with her coffee, waiting for my reply.

"He's Cay. I could never… So, I promise nothing will happen between us while I'm back home."

"So, what I'm hearing is you need to move away to marry him? Great, your bags are already packed, sister-in-law!"

"Why are you encouraging this? I slept with my boss! I'm damaged goods." My stomach sinks remembering what I did.

"Fuck right off with that nonsense. You're *not* damaged goods, and Caleb is a good man. Pretty sure he's been brooding for the past decade since you ruined him with your pussy."

"Cass!" I shriek.

"What?" She raises an eyebrow, taking a drink from her coffee cup that I'm certain is empty at this point. "He doesn't date. There's no harm in casually seeing him while you're home."

I consider it for a moment. He could break my heart—or worse, I could break his again. "It's a bad idea."

"Think about it. I've warned him to stay away from you, but only because I know my brother and I want to torture him. I give it three days before he's on your doorstep, serenading you harder than John Cusack with a boombox."

I gesture with a nod for us to leave my bedroom, and we take a seat on the couch in the living room. Even though we text nearly every day, we spend the next two hours talking and laughing as if we haven't caught up in years. I needed this, needed to be home.

Cass checks the time. "Shit, I have to go open the bar. Want to come to brunch tomorrow?"

"Sure!" She bites back a smile at my reply. "Cass…"

"What?"

"Let me guess, Caleb will be there."

"Maybe," she sings as she gets up, then whines, "Please come? Pop told me to invite you, so you have to say yes."

I roll my eyes. "You win. I'll be there."

# caleb

. . .

I'm off in ten, up for a drink?

INGRID

I'm going to make it an early night.

I'll call you when I get home.

Thank you for last night, but you don't have to.

F*uck that.*

Today must've been hard on her. Once I saw the notifications on my phone with her name plastered all over them, I did what any other obsessed man would do—a full-on internet search of her name. Dozens, if not hundreds, of articles came up. Most appeared to be blatant lies. A few implied she's seeing me… and I selfishly hope those are true.

As soon as I'm in my truck, I call, hoping she'll want me to come by. It rings three times, and just as I'm about to hang up, her sleepy voice gives me pause as my thumb is about to press the 'end' icon.

"Hey, Cay."

I put the phone to my ear, unable to wipe the smile from my face. "Hey, princess. Hope I didn't wake you."

She groans, and there's a shifting of fabric in the background. "No, I'm up. How was work?"

"Good." I fucking hate small talk, but I'll take anything she's willing to give me right now. "Did your boxes arrive yet?"

"Yeah, I haven't unpacked, though."

"Need some help?" I offer, biting my lip and hoping she'll say yes.

"Sure. Have you had dinner?"

It's late, and she's making an effort. My shoulders sag in relief. "No, I'll pick pizza up on the way over."

"You don't have to," she rushes out.

"I know. Text me with your toppings, and I'll be by in a bit."

Thankfully, she doesn't fight me. We hang up, and I wait for a few minutes to order from my buddy's restaurant that opened two weeks ago. When I don't have a text from her, I call in an order for a large pizza with pineapple, even if it makes me cringe. Before I drive, I check my texts, and since I still don't have her topping preferences, I text her, hoping she's not asleep.

> You're getting anchovies.

> Sorry, I was distracted. Your dad came by to pick up his tools.

> Pineapple, please.

I can't help but smile that I had it right. Though the fact that Pop came by has me typing again.

> Tools? He left them in my truck last night.

After driving to the restaurant, I check my phone, finding two missed texts.

> He came by earlier to install a porch swing and left his ratchet set or something.

> Please tell me you didn't get anchovies...

Laughing to myself before I go inside, I reply.

> Extra, just my half.

> Asshole.

I wait a moment, and another text comes in.

> Shit, I'm kidding!

Stuffing my phone back in my pocket, I feel it vibrate a few times. I should answer and reassure her I'm not upset that she called me that, but the pizza is ready, and I want to get on the road. I grab the to-go box and drive to her place. Not wanting to text and drive, as soon as I'm outside the house, I take out my phone.

> I'm sorry. I was kidding.
>
> Seriously, Cay?

*Shit.*

> I'm outside.

I try calling, but she doesn't answer, so I make my way to the front door, pizza in hand. After knocking three times, I hear her footsteps approach. When she opens the door, I'm left speechless—she's somehow more beautiful than last night. Even wearing leggings and an oversized shirt, she's absolutely stunning.

Gripping the back of my neck, I sigh, "You know, you need to stop apologizing when someone else is being a dick."

Her eyes roam my body, landing on my cock before they snap back up to my face. "Sorry, what did you say?"

*Was she checking me out?*

"Stop apologizing when someone else is to blame. What you sent *was* funny, I was just on the road and don't check my messages when I'm driving."

She hums. "Force of habit, I guess."

Ingrid gestures for me to come in, and I make my way to the kitchen island to set down the pizza. When I turn to face her, it takes me a moment, but I notice her hair isn't the usual dark auburn; more of a rich, chocolate brown.

She touches her tied-up hair and offers a sheepish smile. "I needed a change."

I take a step closer, desperate to touch her, hold her... anything she'll afford me. Instead, I fight back the urge and stuff my hands in my pockets. "As long as you like it, that's all that matters." She glances over at the pizza box. "No anchovies, promise."

She bites her lip and lifts the lid, finding the whole pizza is pineapple. "What are you going to eat?"

I stand behind her, looking over her shoulder at the pizza I wouldn't touch with a ten-foot pole. Resisting the obvious flirtatious response, I whisper, "I think I'll manage."

Turning to face me, her back against the counter, lightly biting her lip, she breathes, "You're supposed to say 'you.'"

# ingrid

. . .

I shouldn't be flirting with Caleb; it'll end in disaster. Part of me can't help but wonder if he's *improved* since we slept together. Mostly, I miss him. I miss the easy banter and the way we've always been there for each other. Sure, it's selfish—he's always been mine, even if I've never been his.

I look away, embarrassed at my admission, and mutter, "Sorry, I shouldn't have said that."

Cay tilts my chin until our eyes meet. His voice is soft and reassuring when he insists, "Stop apologizing."

"This is a bad idea." *Even if it feels like the best idea.*

He smiles wide, then leans in until we are only a breath apart, bracing himself on the counter behind me. "For who?"

"Haven't you seen the news?"

"That you fucked your boss and left your job? Pregnant? Or the few where you're mine?"

*If only the last one was true. Fuck, he read them.* I grimace at the admission.

"I don't care." Caleb brushes my hair off my shoulder and whispers beside my ear, "You deserve better, Ingrid." Goosebumps erupt down my arms from his hot breath tickling my neck, and a shiver runs through every inch of me. He pulls back slightly, and just as I think he's going to kiss me, he opens the pizza box wider. "Should I help myself?"

My breath catches, unsure if he's talking about the pizza or me. If he knows why I'm here, and doesn't care that I'm essentially an unemployed slut, he could think I'm an easy lay. My mind is running through the possible options, and as if he can read my mind, he steps away and rounds the island into the kitchen to retrieve plates, giving me space.

*He's talking about the pizza.*

*Just another day in the life of an overthinker.*

I breathe a brief sigh of relief until disappointment settles in my gut. Even after everything, I want him to want me as much as I want him. Taking a plate, I place two slices on it and rummage in the fridge to find the bottle of ranch I purchased this afternoon. Squeezing a dollop on my plate, I notice he's removing the pineapples from his slices, scrunching his nose, and making me laugh.

"Well, you could have ordered pepperoni or something for your half. Want some ranch?" I lift the bottle as an offering.

"Absolutely not." He shudders. "I'll stick with my pineapple-less pizza."

"Suit yourself." I dip my slice in the ranch, take a large, unattractive bite, and let out an exaggerated moan. I mean it as a joke, but his eyes darken. My mouth full, I cover it as I ask, "What?"

His gaze burns into me as he takes a bite of his pizza. When he's done chewing, he finally replies, "I was just thinking I've only heard what you sound like when you're faking it." I suck in a breath. "You think I didn't know?"

"Shit," I whisper. Maybe Martin knew, but didn't care? I've mastered my act over the years, I don't know why I'm doubting myself. But Caleb? Fuck. Shit… Every explicative in the universe.

"That's why it was the worst night of my life." He braces himself on the counter and lowers his head in defeat. My heart lurches; I did this. When he lifts his gaze, he adds, "I'd be lying if I said I didn't want a shot at making it right."

In an instant, my mind is reeling, wondering if this is all it will ever be between us. Maybe he's no different than Martin, or any other man I've been with, for that matter. I can try to rationalize that I wanted it with any of them, that I'm fine with a casual hook-up, sans orgasm.

Not now, not Caleb. I can't do this.

"Ingrid, look at me." When I do, agony is etched on his face. "I'm sorry. I'm fucking this up." He rounds the kitchen island, and I stupidly let him take me in his arms. I wrap mine around his middle, letting him still be my person even if we're both hurting. I can't help but let out a contented sigh being this close to him. "It's not about that. You deserve a man who gives you the world, not just between your legs." I rest my chin on his chest, looking up at him. "Let me be that man until I have to leave."

"One night of you pretending to be my boyfriend?" I laugh. "No, I think I'll pass."

"Three weeks."

My brow furrows. "Three weeks?"

"I ship out in three weeks."

"You, *what?*" I step out of his embrace. No wonder Cass would be fine with something casual between Caleb and me—he's leaving. Any hopes I may have of rekindling whatever this is… officially squashed. "Are you serious?"

"It's my last one, I promised Pop."

"Last what? So, what was your plan here? Make me fall for you and then bail?" The idea has my stomach in knots. What if he doesn't come back?

"It's not like that. I promised another two years before I knew you were coming home." He slides his hand through his hair and rubs the back of his neck. "Fuck, if I had known, I never would've agreed to it."

"So, what now?"

Caleb takes a step forward and closes the distance. "Hurt *me*. Let me fall in love with you, and break my heart."

"No." Shaking my head, I take a step back. "I did once, I won't do it again."

"I survived." He smirks. "Three weeks."

My heart and head are at war. Still, every fiber of me wants to say yes to his ridiculous proposition. "And at the end of three weeks?"

"If I play my cards right, I'll get to keep the girl who got away."

"And you disappear for *years*." I shouldn't care; I left for a decade. But this feels different, *he's* different.

"Ingrid. I've *always* been yours. Give me the chance to show you before I leave." I consider it all. There's no way I'll walk away from this unscathed. He deserves better than this. I deserve better than this. His voice pulls me out of my spiral. "Three weeks?"

"I don't know. Maybe?" I chew on my lip, and he smiles— one that meets his gorgeous brown eyes. My heart can't help melting at the whole declaration. My mind has other ideas. "But we need rules."

"Fine, but you only get three, and I get three. We're not going to write up a whole fucking contract so I can date you."

"All right," I say slowly and carefully. "No sex. I don't want this to get messier than it already is."

"Done," he replies, surprisingly without hesitation. "But I get to stay the night at least once before I leave."

"Clothes on?"

His eyes briefly drag down my body but snap up to meet mine. "Whatever you want."

"Fair. Okay, what's one of yours?"

Cay pauses a moment. "I take you out twice a week."

"That's implied," I laugh.

"*And* you let me kiss you goodnight, wherever you're comfortable."

The implication isn't lost on me, and I cock an eyebrow, crossing my arms over my chest. "I thought I said no sex." He tucks a stray tendril behind my ear, his fingers lingering on my neck as his thumb grazes my jaw. I close my eyes and lean into his touch, covering his hand with mine. "We're idiots for doing this."

"Probably," he chuckles but doesn't pull away. "My second rule: I get your ereader."

"What?" *Record fucking scratch.* My eyes widen. "No deal, I'm out."

"No, you're not. You have all of your paperbacks, and I'll give it back to you in a few weeks... I'm taking it tonight before you can delete books off it."

"I don't read fantasy like I did in high school, Cay," I deadpan.

He leans in and brushes a kiss on my cheek, whispering, "I know, I'm counting on it." His beard tickles, but in a few weeks he'll be clean-shaven. A reminder that if we do this —*really do this*—I only get a short time with him. I need to make the most of it. My hands slide down his chest, and it vibrates beneath my fingertips as he groans.

"The pizza's getting cold," I whisper, my eyes fixed on his toned pecs, wondering if they look as good as they feel. He's in incredible shape, and I am, well... not.

"I'm not hungry," he says cooly.

"I should unpack."

"Probably."

A silent moment passes between us, and I finally look up. He's still the same man I wanted desperately for years, only we're all grown up now, and I still want him. "Fuck it." I lift onto my toes and kiss him. It takes him by surprise, and his fingers tangle in my hair tugging gently to pull me back until our lips are only brushing. "What?"

"You asked for rules," he laughs. "I gave you two of mine, but I only have one of yours." Cay kisses my neck, and a whine escapes me. Already wanting to retract my first and only rule, if we did sleep together, I know it would be nothing like the last time. He'll ruin me. I deserve it after breaking his heart and hiding my secrets from him.

"Oh, right." I can barely think, enjoying the contrast of his rough beard and soft lips on my neck. He nips at my earlobe, making me moan, imagining his mouth everywhere he didn't kiss me last time. I'd give anything for a chance to fix things between us, even if I only get a few weeks.

"While you come up with an arbitrary rule that we'll throw out at some point, my final one is that you'll never fake anything with me again. If I ever have the pleasure of your thighs keeping my ears warm, I want you to make a mess all over my face, begging for more."

*Has he been reading my books? He's giving off severe book-boyfriend energy right now. Is that why he wants my ereader?*

"Cay, I—"

"Need to unpack. Great idea."

He presses a final kiss to my neck and makes his way into the spare bedroom. There's an empty floor-to-ceiling bookcase and no less than six large moving boxes scattered against the other walls. He shuffles them around and opens them, finding my collection of everything from classics to monster romance.

"I know, there are too many," I sigh. "They'll never fit."

He looks up and smirks. "Oh, we'll make them fit."

# caleb

. . .

The sun peeks in through the curtains, too bright to open my eyes. *Fuck, what time is it?* It takes me a moment to register my surroundings—my arm is numb, there's a weight on half my body that isn't normally there, the faint smell of daffodils, and... the sigh of a woman?

My eyes fly wide, and I glance down, finding Ingrid curled up against me, her leg slung over mine, cheek and palm resting on my chest. A paperback and ereader on the other side of me... *We must've fallen asleep reading last night.* I can't help but smile; I'd give anything to wake up to her every morning, just like this.

Unable to resist, I kiss the top of her head, and she hums in response, pulling closer to me. "I take it back," she mutters sleepily.

"Hmm?"

"Rules are stupid." Her voice is muffled by my chest, but my cock is a bit too excited at the suggestion, hearing it loud and fucking clear.

"I like my rules," I tease. "You only have one, by the way."

Sliding her hand down to my stomach, within an inch of my hard cock, she whispers, "Can I change it?"

I tilt her chin and lean in to brush a soft kiss to her lips, wondering how much she'll let me have of her. She sighs a whimper as I pull back, and I try my fucking hardest to not read too much into it. "What do you want to change it to?"

"We should have a bucket list instead," Ingrid answers matter-of-factly. "First on the list, I want you to break my heart, not the other way around."

"No," I growl and she laughs. "Absolutely not."

"Hear me out! I've never been in love before, and, well… for once, I want to fall head-over-heels, madly in love. I want to know what it feels like to have your heart ripped out. To cry for a solid month when you have to leave. Can you make that happen?"

The woman I've wanted for most of my life shifts and straddles me, my hands instinctively gripping her thighs, wanting to tempt fate.

*Who the fuck thought it was a good idea to stay the night with a beautiful woman wearing just her underwear and a tee?*

*Oh, right, me.*

*Fucking. Idiot.*

"What are you up to, princess?"

She shakes her head and scrunches her nose. "Princess? You'll need to get more creative than that."

"Ingrid doesn't have a lot of nickname options, you know," I chuckle. She doesn't find it funny, instead, she rolls her hips and grinds against me. I stifle a groan, but a hiss still escapes. "Really? That's how you want this to go?" I flip her onto her back, and she lets out a full laugh that I feel everywhere. *This* is how it was how it was supposed to be.

"You're the one that insists on calling me princess. Which, by the way, feels a little condescending."

"And here I thought it was endearing." I give her a taste of her own medicine. Still in boxer briefs, I rub the length of my cock against her now-wet panties. She grasps the sheets and arches her back, making it that much harder for me to keep control. "Would you say last night was a date?"

"I guess? Why?" she manages, her breath already broken and ragged.

"I was promised that I would get to kiss you goodnight." I lean in until our lips are nearly touching, noses brushing, and remind her, "*Anywhere* you'll let me."

"It's morning," she whispers.

"Does that mean I get breakfast before we have brunch?"

"Brunch!" she shrieks, startling me. "Shit, we're supposed to have brunch with your dad and Cass!"

My face falls to the crook of her neck as I laugh. "You're not going to make this easy on me, are you?"

"What do you… *Oh!* Yeah. I didn't pick up on that little breakfast joke. It was a good one, too!"

Unable to tear my lips from her neck, I murmur against her skin, "With what you read? I figured you'd be quicker to pick up on it." I'm fucking addicted to the taste of her.

Sliding my hand up her side until I reach her full breast, I tease her taut nipple with my thumb as I suck harder on her neck, enough to leave a dark red mark. She moans at my touch and, *fuck,* it's the sweetest sound I've ever heard. Not only do I want to make up for our shitty one night together, I want to selfishly ruin her for any other man. This won't be three weeks, I want to keep her, always.

"What do you want, Ingrid?" I purr, desperate for her to let me taste every last inch of her.

"I… I don't know," she answers honestly. I pull back, but she cups my neck and tugs me closer until my lips are back on her. "You can keep doing that, though."

I chuckle and tug back a second time, gripping her wrist and pinning it above her head before she can pull me down again. I know it's my ego that I should've left at the door, but I want her to come… right fucking now. I need to know what it feels like to have her riding my face or her pussy clenching around my fingers as I taste her. I was a selfish prick when we were younger, and it wasn't until a year or so later that I realized she didn't actually come, it was all a show. This time, I want all of her. No performance.

"My third rule was that you'll never fake anything with me. Fuck, I want to touch you, but I need to know that you'll tell me to stop if something's too much or if you need more."

She chews on her lip and whispers, "Okay."

"Okay isn't good enough," I insist, nearly calling her princess. She's right, she isn't one—she's a damn goddess. My jaw tics at the thought of anything mediocre with her.

"Yes." Ingrid draws her lips into her mouth, smothering her smile. I can't help myself and close the distance, kissing her as if it's our last. It's raw and a little frenzied, as if both of us were holding out for this moment for years. Her fingers dimple my back, pulling me closer, and no matter how good it feels, I force back any thoughts of sinking myself inside her this morning.

Trailing kisses down her neck, I land on the small mark I left, grazing my teeth against it. Her gasps and moans become louder as she tangles her fingers in my hair, guiding me lower. While she won't tell me what she wants, I love that she's showing me. Lifting up her shirt, I kiss her soft stomach, making her hips buck once. I grip them tightly, holding her in place, and groan, "I've waited years to make up for that night. There's no need to rush. You're going to let me enjoy myself."

"Okay," she whimpers.

I slide my hand up her shirt and cup her breast, pinching her nipple hard enough to make her yelp. "I thought I said okay isn't good enough?"

"Yes," she breathes.

*Fuck, she listens so fucking beautifully.*

I pinch harder this time, and she lets out a delicious moan, her eyes fluttering closed in ecstasy. I missed this last time, but I sure as fuck won't again. She's so fucking perfect when she's relaxed like this, but I need more. Lifting her shirt higher, I move back up her body, peppering kisses until my lips seal around one of her nipples, swirling my tongue twice, then sucking hard. As I pull back a little, I keep it between my teeth, making her grip the sheets tighter beneath us.

"Doing *okay?*" I tease, moving to the other side.

I continue my torture and she pants, "Yeah." Slipping my fingers into the waistband of her panties, I pull down an inch, but she grabs both of my wrists. "We don't have to do this. I need a shower and"—I pull down another inch—"I'm due for a wax."

"The city boys you've been with may care, but I sure as fuck don't." I sit back on my heels, admiring my dream come true lying before me. My voice softer, I insist, "Tell me to stop, and I will. Otherwise, I'm not going to until you come for me."

I tear the fabric and toss it to the ground. Her hands fly to her face in embarrassment, but I pull them away and kiss the inside of one of her palms. While she hasn't told me what was true or not from the news articles, if there's the smallest chance she was taken advantage of, I refuse to have her ever feel that way about me.

"You're in control here, not me. This can end right now and nothing will change." I place her palm on my chest above my heart. "I'd happily stay every night with you for the next decade and never touch you, if that's what you wanted."

Ingrid lifts onto her elbows. "What if you can't make me come? And you spend an hour doing the Lord's work down there, for nothing? We miss brunch, it becomes highly suspicious that we're both missing. Oh, and I'm pretty sure you left a giant hickey on my neck. Cass will see, she'll start wedding planning, and—" I kiss her, stopping her spiral of hypotheticals. "What if, Cay?"

"What if we make our own rules, our own bucket list? Who cares what my sister or Pop thinks? Who cares what the media thinks?" I grab my phone from the bedside table and set a timer for three minutes. "You're worried about timing? When I wanted to become a SEAL, I was tested to see how long I could hold my breath. I needed to last two to three minutes underwater. Even though I failed one of the other tests, I lasted the full three." I hover my thumb over the 'start' button. "Give me three minutes to try."

"Are you su—"

"Yes."

Ingrid covers my hand, pauses for a moment, then presses the start button. "Three minutes."

I waste no time sliding down her body and slinging her legs over my shoulders. With only three minutes, I don't have enough confidence with my tongue alone, reinforcements are needed.

Licking once up her center, I'm instantly drunk from the taste of her. It takes me a moment to recover. If I wasn't a dumbass in high school, I could've been living between her legs with her thighs as earmuffs for the last decade. The realization hurts more than I thought it would.

After sliding two fingers up and down her slit twice, I finally press into her; curling right where she needs me with my tongue continuing to circle her clit. Her breathy moans fill the room, and I do my best to avoid looking at the clock at all cost.

*She's here. She wants me. She's mine.*

I continue the same pace and pressure of my tongue, but it's not enough for her. My fingers massage the one spot that should have her come undone... Nothing.

*Shit!*

*Time is running out and I refuse to lose.*

I kiss up her body, keeping my fingers deep inside her. I kiss her once, then beg a little too desperately, "Tell me. What do you need?"

"More," she replies breathlessly. I press a third finger inside her, making her gasp, and increase the pressure of my tongue.

It only takes a minute and a half before she moans, "Right there, don't stop... Oh, fuck... *Cay*," with her perfect pussy clenching tighter around my fingers. She isn't just tight, though, there's a pulsing as she cries out, giving me pause. My beard is fucking soaked, the bed even wetter. She may be able to fake moaning, but there's no denying that I made her come this time. I suck harder, making her scream in pleasure, not wanting the three minutes to end.

Unfortunately, the timer on my phone beeps.

"Cay, I"—I nip at her thigh—"*fuck*."

*Mine.*

I take my time kissing up her body until I reach her lips. I pull down my boxers a few inches and slide my cock inside her, and a soft moan escapes her. Pushing in to the hilt, I take a moment to savor the feeling of her perfect pussy wrapped around it. Sex will wait for another day, but I need to feel her right now, for as long as she'll let me.

# ingrid

. . .

D*id we just have sex?*
*No…*

*His cock is inside me… but we didn't have sex.*

*But that was…*

*Fuck, it felt good.*

*It wasn't earth-shattering, but I came.*

*Can we do that again?*

*Does he want to do it again?*

*Oh shit! He didn't come!*

"Ingrid." His soothing voice pulls me from my thoughts.

"Yeah?"

"You can't keep grinding on me like that, or I'll come."

I'm still in a daze, hardly processing his words when mine
tumble from my lips, "Good."

Caleb brushes a few mussed locks away before pressing a soft kiss to my forehead. "As much as I want to, I'm bare. Do you have any condoms?"

"In some random box I packed," I grumble, kicking myself for not having a few loose ones in my purse. After what happened last time, we should be careful. As he slowly pulls his cock out, I feel empty—not just physically. "Cay…"

"We're even." Rolling to the side, he fluffs the pillow and lays facing me. There isn't an ounce of regret in his features, he actually appears… happy? "We need to leave in a bit, mind if I take a quick shower?"

"Oh, sure, go ahead." I wave him off, still coming down from my high.

His boyish grin widens. "Let me rephrase that. Come take a quick shower *with* me."

Caleb slinks off the bed, removes his boxer briefs the rest of the way, and grips the nape of his shirt, pulling it over his head. Embarrassment washes over me as I ogle this Adonis standing before me.

*Was it 'ab day' every day at the gym, or something? Nope, it was also 'arm day'… and 'leg day'…*

"Ingrid." My eyes snap away from appreciating his perfectly sculpted body to meet his gaze.

I blink twice. *Shit! He caught me checking him out.* Despite still wearing a shirt, I self-consciously grasp the comforter to hide my significantly softer body, and pull it up to my chin. "Enjoy your shower."

With a devilish smirk, he grips the comforter and tugs it off me. "*We* are going to enjoy a shower."

"Nope," I insist, popping the 'p,' and scrambling to find my underwear, only to find them shredded on the ground. "I'll take one later."

In a swift motion, he grabs my ankles and pulls me until my ass is almost hanging off the bed, making me squeal. Leaning in, bracing himself with his hands on either side of me, he chuckles darkly, "That's the last time you hide your beautiful body from me, understood?" He traces the mark on my neck, and my breath catches. "No faking, no hiding."

"I think that's more than three rules." Lifting off the bed, he offers his hand, but I don't take it. Instead, not tearing my eyes away from his, I pull my shirt off and toss it to the ground. Admittedly, I'm a bit disappointed there was no 'good fucking girl' to accompany it, but I'm quickly distracted by his hand falling to his cock that is so damn hard, begging to be touched, licked, sucked…

"Don't get any ideas, Ingrid." Caleb tilts my chin, forcing my gaze up. "Shower, then brunch."

I stand, acutely aware of our size difference; it's a stark contrast to when we were younger, he didn't have muscles on top of muscles. Playfully, I narrow my eyes, and he mirrors me, though he's unable to hide his adorable boyish grin. Before I can get a word out, he bends and lifts me up and over his shoulder, stalking off to the bathroom.

"Cay! Put me down! You're going to throw your back out, and the Navy will arrest me for putting an officer on bedrest."

When we reach the shower, he slides me down his body until my feet hit the floor but keeps me flush against him. "I never told you I was an officer."

"I may or may not have internet stalked you yesterday." Reaching around him, I turn on the shower. "If I take a shower with you"—I bite my lip and sigh—"we won't be going to brunch."

"We're doing both." Caleb walks me backward into the shower, the scalding hot water pouring down on us. He sucks in a breath, then mutters, "Fuck, that's hot." I turn the knob, keeping the water warm enough to steam around us, but not enough to burn.

I'm sure I look like a drowned rat. It doesn't stop him from taking my face in my hands and kissing me roughly.

All of this feels like a dream. Maybe when I was in Martin's office, I dissociated a little too hard? I can only hope that I don't wake up from whatever this is. It's going to hurt like hell when Caleb leaves, but I want to savor every last moment I have with him. I deserve to have him break my heart, especially after everything that happened.

We never had sweet moments like this when we were younger; I was too scared of losing Cass *and* Cay. It was foolish to consider 'what ifs' when he was leaving for the Navy out of high school, and I was off to college. In a few weeks, he'll be gone again, but I selfishly want to pretend he's not. There's no harm in kissing this beautiful, amazing man every chance I get… *right?*

The water beats down on both of us, and I can't get close enough. For years, I survived without him and Cass, avoiding coming home for Christmas and summer breaks.

The moment my parents moved away from here, I had the perfect excuse to never return.

My career took off right after college, earning me a seat at the table of one of the biggest shows on the network. Within a few years, I moved up the ranks, but if I'm being honest with myself, I'd throw it all away if it meant I could start all over with Cay.

Jokes on me; that's exactly what I'm doing. I walked away from years of late nights and friendships pushed to the back burner. I don't know if I'll ever write again. Right now, in this moment, I honestly couldn't care less. I allow the water to wash away any regrets I'm holding onto, and let the most incredible man I've ever known to kiss me.

But guilt gets the best of me, and it'll only get harder to tell him the truth later. "Cay, I have to tell you something." I take his face in my hands and tear my lips away. "I understand if you never want to speak to me again after what I'm about to say but... that night, I didn't just lose my virginity." He waits patiently, covering my hands and kissing my palms, while I try to muster the courage to get the words out. "A month after you left, I was rushed by my parents to the doctors, because I was in severe pain and couldn't stop bleeding."

"Fuck, are you ok? What happened? Why didn't you tell me? Did Cass—"

I silence his questions with my finger to his lips, but his eyes are still so full of worry. Tears I held back for years threaten to fall, but I hold them back. "No one knew, just my parents. *Fuck*, this is so hard to say out loud." I shut my eyes tightly, not wanting to see his reaction. "I lost our baby, Cay." I feel him step back so I open my eyes, pain etched on each and every one of his features. "I missed one period. I thought it was stress. I didn't know until it was too late. I'm so—"

Caleb cuts off my words with a searing kiss full of love, pain, and regret. "Don't you dare apologize."

I don't listen. "I'm sorry, I should've told you."

Caleb drops to his knees, and this sweet, perfect man who I don't deserve, kisses my stomach. He looks up at me, and I brush the wet locks off his forehead. "I'm sorry I wasn't there."

So much anguish flashes in his eyes that I slink down the shower wall, meeting his kneel. He wraps his arms tightly around me. Nestling his face in the crook of my neck, he says something that sounds a hell of a lot like 'I love you.'

*He doesn't, he couldn't.*

Silence passes as steam envelops us until he finally breaks it. "How am I going to leave you for two years when I have you right here, in my arms? You were my *everything*. I... I can't lose you when I leave."

"You'll survive," I tease, throwing his words back at him, but don't let go of him.

"I lied."

"Cay..."

"No." He pulls back, and a rogue tear leaves my eye, for the third time in ten years. I just hope it's masked enough through the shower water. "We were supposed to be a family. Maybe it wasn't our time then, and sure, I'd be lying if I said I didn't want that with you now. But how am I supposed to let you go when I leave?" He kisses me, but instead of the fire from earlier, it's full of fear, as if his lips may never touch mine again.

Between kisses, I whisper, "You survived. I survived. *We* survived, Cay." Weighing heavy on my heart, I admit, "I haven't seen you in years. You were always mine, but I was never yours. Maybe this time, we do things differently?"

Caleb pulls back and tenderly kisses my forehead, breathing a contented sigh. All of this is so heavy, but I've never felt lighter. Even though he's leaving for a couple of years, I can visit, maybe even move closer to the base.

*What the fuck am I saying? I've been back one day, and I'm forcing myself into his life.*

"Get out of your head, Ingrid," he laughs and I chuckle softly.

"Busted."

"Let me get you cleaned up and a proper breakfast in you. We can figure out the rest later."

# caleb

. . .

I normally look forward to Sunday brunch, but I'm worried about what Cass or Pop will say when I come strolling in with Ingrid after they both warned me to take things slowly with her. They have to know I'd never listen. This is Ingrid, there's no way in hell I'd be able to stay away.

We pull up to the house, and the moment I turn the ignition off, Ingrid pivots to face me. "No faking, no hiding," she says confidently, but then meekly adds, "Unless"—she chews on her lip and looks down at her wringing hands— "you don't want to tell them."

Covering her hands with one of mine, she looks up. "No faking, no hiding. Pop will give me shit about it later, maybe Cass will, too. I don't care." I bring her fingers to my lips, brushing a gentle kiss to her knuckles. "Ready?" She blows out a long breath and nods.

Hopping out of the truck, I expect her stubborn, independent streak to shine through and open her own door. I take the small win that she lets me do it for her. As I shut the door, I press her against it, sliding my hand into her hair and bringing her lips to mine—I need one last taste of her.

Ingrid sighs a whimpered moan as we break apart, and I can't help the stupid grin plastered on my face—she was always supposed to be mine.

She takes my hand, and we make our way up to the front door. As she's about to knock, I open it wide to the smell of fresh waffles and the crackling of cooked bacon filling the house.

"Pop?"

"Get your ass in here. You're late," he calls from the kitchen. We continue further into the house, finding him sipping a mimosa in a pint glass that's more champagne than orange juice and placing a tray of waffles in the oven to keep warm. "I want to talk to you before Cass and Ingrid show—" He turns and spots us. "Oh. You're here."

"Need a hand?" Ingrid offers and helps herself to a pint glass from the cabinet. She sets it next to his and pours nearly half the bottle into hers, topping it off with a splash of orange juice. "Cheers." They clink their glasses and both take long drinks, making Pop laugh.

I clear my throat. They look over, shrug, and continue. "Really?"

Pop finishes his, then does a double-take of my clothes, a scowl now replacing his smile. "Didn't you wear that yesterday?"

I glance down at my shirt and jeans, raking my hand through my hair. "Oh, yeah, I guess I did." He looks at

Ingrid—who's flushed from champagne and embarrassment—and back at me, his jaw tight.

"Let me start the waffles," Ingrid rushes out.

"Everything's done, just need to wash the blueberries."

"Blueberries?" she squeals in excitement. "Are they from the St. Clair's?"

"Of course! Ashlyn now sells them at the Saturday farmers market when she's off-duty. Since she had to work yesterday, she offered to drop them off last night."

He gestures with a nod toward the sink, and Ingrid spots them immediately, practically skipping to them. While she rinses them off, she plops a couple in her mouth and lets out the sweetest moan that has my cock standing at attention. I quickly adjust, but Pop catches me.

"What did I tell you?" he grumbles.

"It's fine," I assure him, but his glare doesn't let up.

"No, it's not. You'd marry her today if you could, then drag her all the way to the other side of the country with you, just for them to throw you on a sub for who the fuck knows how long."

"Oh, she'll come." My voice is a little too loud, and Ingrid looks over her shoulder, the blood draining from her face. "To, um… San Diego," I add, stifling a laugh, and she continues washing the berries and laying them out to dry. Thankfully, Pop didn't catch it.

Ingrid grabs her mimosa and asks, "What's this about San Diego?"

"It's where they're thinking of sending Caleb in *three weeks*," Pop answers before I can; the emphasis isn't lost on me. We both know this is fucking stupid, but I can't help myself. This isn't a random woman I met; it's Ingrid Fucking Lawrence. "That's if they don't put him on a ship or a sub."

"The party has arriv—" Cass sets a bottle of champagne down on the counter. "Who died?"

"No one, sweetheart." Pop wraps Cass in a tight hug. "I'm giving your brother shit for leaving."

"Again? Typical Sunday, I see," she laughs, steps out of his hold, then kisses Ingrid on the cheek. Cass whispers something that has Ingrid's eyes wide and cheeks crimson.

"Now what?" I groan.

"I was right," Cass sings and lifts onto her toes, reaching to ruffle my hair like I'm a fucking child. "How was the serenade, dearest brother? Put Johnny to shame? Please tell me there was a trench coat."

"There was no serenading," Ingrid rushes out, but Cass isn't fazed.

"Ooo, Ashlyn must've popped by." Cassidy tosses a few blueberries into her mouth, and when none of us reply, her hands go to her hips. "What's going on? My best friend is here for the first time in years, and you all look sad as fuck."

"She's right." Pop pulls out the bacon, sausage, and waffles he was keeping warm in the oven, then takes a seat at the kitchen table. "Dig in before it gets cold." Cassidy joins him and pulls out her phone, typing something.

Ingrid rushes to the cabinet, but I beat her to it and remove four plates, setting them on the counter next to the food. Just like when we were younger, I watch as she plates two waffles, four strips of bacon, and three sausage links, then fills each crevice of the waffle with a blueberry.

As she works on her masterpiece, she asks, "Where do you keep the syrup?"

I rummage through the pantry to find the small jug of maple syrup for her. Stepping behind her, I set the syrup on the counter, sliding my free hand around her waist and pulling her flush with me.

With my fingers splayed on Ingrid's stomach, I press a single kiss to her neck, and she hisses, "Your dad's right there."

"When we get home, you're giving me more than three minutes," I whisper, nipping at her earlobe.

Shimmying out of my hold, she adds a drizzle of syrup to the waffles, walks over to the table, and sets the plate in front of Pop.

"Suck up," Cass teases Ingrid as she gets up to fill her plate. "So, what's the plan for today?"

I load up a plate identical to Pop's for Ingrid, and reply, "I was going to take Ingrid out on the lake later." Ingrid takes the last plate, assuming the one in my hand isn't for her. I snatch it from her, nestle it under the one I'm filling, and insist, "Go sit down."

"I can get my own, you know." Rolling her eyes, she lifts her hand expectantly, but I continue preparing her plate, and top off her glass with orange juice. "Really, Cay?"

I guide her by the small of her back to the table and set the plates down to pull out her chair. She reluctantly takes a seat, grumbling something under her breath, but she gives in and sighs, "Thank you."

Pop and Ingrid dig in as Cass and I grab our food. As I hand the tongs for the bacon to Cass, she whispers, "Did she tell you?"

Ingrid claimed Cass didn't know about her miscarriage, so I coolly ask, "Tell me what?"

"About what happened in New York? You think I didn't see that sneaky little moment? You need to step up your game if you want to win over my best friend before you leave."

"Okay, I'm listening…"

"I'm talking doorway leans, gray sweatpants, the works. Get a damn puppy, if you have to. Look, I don't want either of you to get hurt, and please be careful with her. She's had the week from hell after her boss… *was an asshole*. She deserves a good guy. And maybe convince her to stay." Cass then paints on a fake smile and takes a bite of her bacon before joining Ingrid and Pop.

With everything that's happened, I've ignored the fact that there's a reason Ingrid's here—and it's not because of me. I know my sister means well, but her ominous warnings just make things worse.

Once we're all seated at the table, Cassidy breaks the silence, "What time are we going on the lake?"

"We?" I frown.

Cass takes a large bite of her waffles and purposely takes longer to chew than necessary. "You said we were going on the lake later."

"I said I was taking *Ingrid*, not you."

"Um, hi." Ingrid raises her hand. "No one asked me if I wanted to go on a boat."

"You up for going out later?" I know the answer, but I can't help making light of it.

Ingrid raises an indignant chin. "I have plans." Disappointment hits me as she busies herself with her breakfast, but I lean back in my chair expectantly, waiting to hear what these faux plans are. She finally looks over with an undeniable smirk. "I'm making a bucket list."

"Yes!" Cass cheers. "We should have a bucket list while you're back. I've been dying to go antiquing in Linton and take one of the flower arrangement classes Dani puts on." I chose the wrong time to take a sip of Ingrid's mimosa and nearly spit it out. Ingrid, still eating, covers her mouth as she tries to keep from laughing. "There's nothing funny about that. We should do it!"

"What's on your list, Ingrid?" Pop looks at us incredulously, but it only makes Ingrid and I laugh harder.

When her giggles don't subside, I answer for her, "We haven't decided but she said she wanted to do as much as we can before I leave."

Cass turns toward me and covers half her face, mouthing, "Gross," no doubt having figured out exactly what kind of bucket list I'm referring to. She turns back and asks Ingrid, "What's first on the list?"

"Well… other than spending time with all of you, I want to pitch a new show idea and get hired by another network, once the media storm dies down a bit."

Her answer takes me by surprise. "What's it about?"

Ingrid leans in and whispers, "It's a secret."

We spend the remainder of breakfast with Pop listening to Ingrid tell him about her time in New York; Cass and I comparing notes on a book she finished reading; Cassidy begging Ingrid to take a trip to Los Angeles if and when she pitches her idea… And all the while, I sit back and enjoy the easy banter between my family and the one woman who will always fit in here. There will only be a couple more Sunday brunches before I need to leave, and I know I'll be counting down the days until I'm able to get back here. I need to find a way to keep her. Cass is right, though, I need to be careful until Ingrid shares why she's back.

After breakfast, Cass and Pop are on the back porch, while Ingrid and I clean up and wash the dishes that piled up in the sink. It's all too easy with her, and I can't help wondering what it would take for her to come with me in a few weeks.

Comfortable silence passes between us while I wash and she dries. As I finish with the last plate, I lean against the counter and dry my hands with a kitchen towel. She wipes the excess water from the plate and places it in the rack, then glances up, catching me staring.

Ingrid mirrors my stance and narrows her eyes. When I don't budge, she lifts onto her toes and kisses my cheek. As she falls back onto her heels, unable to help myself, I check that Cass and Pop are still busy, then grip the front of Ingrid's delicate throat and bring her lips to mine. Our kisses are unrushed as my tongue sweeps across hers, loving the taste of orange and sweet blueberry lingering from breakfast. She slides her hands up my sides under my shirt, forcing a groan from me. It's nearly my undoing.

With a soft chuckle, she mutters against my lips, "What's first on your list?"

I pull back and graze my thumb along her jaw, lost in her eyes. "Wrestle a shark, maybe fight a bear…" Ingrid's full laugh fills the kitchen until I admit, "My list begins and ends with you."

I expect a swoon, but her face falls. "What happens when you leave?"

*I get to spend forever with you.*

"We'll find out, together." I press a final kiss to her lips.

*No matter what, I'll always be hers.*

# ingrid
. . .

"I don't know how to do this," I grumble, attempting to untie the pontoon boat from the dock.

Caleb steps out of the boat, laughing, "You said you knew how! Are you sure you're not a princess?"

"It didn't look difficult!"

He swiftly pulls the rope from the anchor and then ushers me into the boat. "Get in, Your Majesty. We're adding knots to your bucket list."

I roll my eyes but do as he asks, carefully boarding. Growing up, I was more of an 'eat snacks and read on the boat' girl, never having to worry about anchors, gear shifts, or what type of fuel a boat needs. Knots? No fucking idea.

Glancing out onto the water, he notes, "It's a bit choppy today, so we should have the lake to ourselves." Starting the motor, we push off from the dock, and the cool lake air whips around me. "Fuck, Ingrid. You had to wear that?"

I look down at my sundress, which is currently mimicking Marilyn Monroe's steam vent moment. I grip the sides and sit on the closest seat. "What? It's hot today…"

"You've been in the city too long. You know damn well it gets windy on the water."

*Oh, I'm well aware of what to expect on the lake.*

Stolen glances, innocent touches, occasional flirting. I miss it. When we were younger, he'd look at me with heat and hunger in his eyes. The way he looks at me now, there's love, etched with pain… but no fire. I was selfishly hoping that by showing a little skin, I'd see it again. Instead of itching to rip my dress off me, he's growling like a dad wanting teenage me to cover up.

Caleb takes us around one of the banks and out of sight of the other boats, then slows his speed and turns the motor off. "The water is too rough today to go further out," he explains, dropping the anchor.

"Why are we out here, then?"

"Come here."

I get up and make my way to him, my dress lifting sporadically with the wind. Beneath his sunglasses and hat, I can't gauge his reaction. I stand between his legs, biting my lip as he takes his hat off. After a quick rake of his hair, puts his cap on backward, and slowly slides his hands up the sides of my dress.

"Fuck." He traces the waistband of my swim bottoms. "Do you have any idea how hard it is to keep my hands to myself with you?"

I take off his sunglasses and set them in the cup holder, still waiting to see the fire in his honey-brown eyes. I'm nothing if not determined, though this feels like a game of chicken I'm going to lose. This dress was a mistake, but only because he wasn't wrong about the lake—it's freezing.

Caleb slides his palms to my ass and pulls me closer. His grip is firm, but it's as if he's holding back. Cautious. I don't want any of it. I've spent most of my life running from whatever this is between us, and when I'm ready to give in—ready for *us* to give in—he's taking his time. Even if it's only for a few weeks, I want to pretend he's mine.

Keeping one hand firmly on my ass, his other follows the outline of my swimsuit bottom around my hip until his fingers are dipping dangerously close to where I desperately want him. I can't take the teasing and press against him, wishing with all of my being that he'll touch me. I don't have to wait long, gasping as his fingers slip under the fabric and press inside me.

A soft moan escapes me as I whisper, "You know, if you can't keep your hands to yourself, maybe it's time I learn how to tie a proper knot?"

He presses another finger inside me. "Come for me, and I'll show you."

"Show me, and I'll come for you," I counter, clenching my pussy around his fingers.

"So fucking stubborn." Pulling out of me, he brings his fingers to my lips and commands, "Open, princess." I do as he asks—even though I'm not loving the pet name—and he slides his coated fingers along my tongue. I close my lips around them and suck them clean, enjoying the flicker I've been craving dancing in his eyes. He closes the distance and kisses me—unexpectedly soft and sweet. The passion I yearn for is definitely there, full of…

*Oh, fuck. He's making love to my mouth.*

*And I'm letting him?*

*When I told him to make me fall in love with him, I think he took me seriously.*

His kisses are languid, sensual… fucking exquisite. With each swipe of his tongue against mine, I'm quickly losing control of the situation. When we break apart, he guides me back a step and falls to one knee. Shivers cascade down my limbs as his hands slide under my dress again, this time to remove my swimsuit bottoms.

"I thought you were going to teach me how to tie a proper knot," I taunt. As he stands, he stuffs them in his pocket, and I'm unable to tear my eyes away from him.

"You don't need underwear to tie a knot." About to kiss me, he notices the goosebumps on my arms. "Damn it, Ingrid, you're freezing." He takes off his long-sleeved flannel shirt and helps me slip it on. His scowl softens, replaced with a a boyish grin that meets his eyes. "Fuck, you look good in my clothes." I can't help returning his smile as I wrap it tighter around me. He reaches into his bag, pulling out nylon rope that's thinner than the one attached to the anchor. Sitting back in his seat, I resume my place between his legs and unravel half of it. "Perfect. That's enough. So, this one you can use for anything you need a loop for."

"Like your hands?"

It earns me a small chuckle. "Yeah, like my hands. Here, I'll show you." I excitedly offer my wrists, and he creates a small loop in the rope. "You'll overlap the rope here, slip the slack through the hole." He wraps the rope around my wrists and slips it into the small loop where he overlapped it. "Loop around like this, and back into the hole." He pulls it tight, and I'm unable to free my hands. "Bowline." Like magic, he unties me and reaches into his bag again, this time pulling out a tactical knife. "Just in case."

Caleb offers his wrists willingly and walks me through the same steps. When I pull it tight, I squeal, "I did it!"

Even though his hands are tied, he manages to grab a fistful of my dress and pulls me closer. "And now you're going to use me to come."

# caleb

. . .

"Well, with you all tied up, I certainly could have my way with you... And there's nothing you could do about it," Ingrid taunts, lightly biting her lip, beckoning me to take it between my teeth. I resist.

I don't have the heart to break it to her that I could easily slip out of the rope. As much as I loved being inside her this morning, I'm playing for keeps. Ingrid hasn't shared what happened in New York, but I have a feeling someone hurt her. If they did, I want to prove that I will give her whatever she needs—with literal and metaphorical hands tied.

Falling to her knees, she unbuckles my cargo shorts, and slowly unzips them. Looking up at me with doe eyes, a growl gets stuck in my throat as she attempts to shimmy them down my hips. Pretending to be retrained is going to be harder than I thought. Her face scrunches at her failed attempt, and it's fucking adorable. I stand for her to pull them down, and sit once she has my cock free. She doesn't move, her eyes fixed on it. When she finally looks up, a devilish smirk appears, and my eyes narrow.

"What are you up—" She licks from my balls to the tip, swirling her tongue a few times before taking all of me in her mouth. "*Fuck.* I thought I told you to use me to come, not fuck me with your mouth."

Ingrid pulls her warm mouth off me to smugly insist, "What are you going to do about it?"

My hands still joined, albeit poorly, I grip her chin before she can wrap her mouth around me again. "That's not how this works. Making you come for me is enough. It'll have to be, because I'm not having sex with you." I drag my thumb along her bottom lip. "That includes your mouth."

"What are you talking about? We had sex this morning." She kisses the pad of my thumb, and I nearly retract everything as she rests her head on my thigh. The most beautiful woman in the world is on her knees for me, and I'm playing it safe. I need to remind myself that she wasn't mine back then, and still isn't now.

"No, just because you came, doesn't mean we had sex. It's not the same thing."

Ingrid laughs, "By that logic, we didn't have sex when we were younger, either."

"You know what I mean." She rolls her eyes, and I continue, "I want to do more than taste and touch you." I help her up and graze my knuckle against her clit through her dress as she stands, making her shiver. I don't want her to feel rejected, but I need more, I want all of her. "I need to know what happened in New York, first."

Ingrid takes a step back and looks away. *Fuck.* I pushed her too hard, too fast, and it's all backfiring. Her voice soft, she sighs, "I don't want to talk about it." Through with the tied-up charade, I slip out of the rope. "Hey!"

I stand, but still give her space, pulling up my pants, and fastening them. "I know you've only been back for a couple of days, and I'm probably asking a lot of you, but I need this to be real between us. I know I said I didn't care what was true or not. You don't have to give me details, I just... I need to know if it was serious with the guy at the network. Am I just a rebound for you?"

Her eyes snap up and immediately find mine. "Cay, no. Absolutely not." She closes the distance and wraps her arms around me, pressing her cheek on my chest. My arms instinctively envelop her, and as I kiss the top of her head, she offers, "I'll tell you one day. I promise. But, you are not and never will be a rebound."

As much as it pains me to ask, I do anyway, "Did someone hurt you?"

"What are you going to do?" she chuckles against me. "Change power dynamics globally so men don't abuse their positions?"

*Is that what happened? Did her boss take advantage of her?*

"Say the word, princess, and I'll slay the dragon." While I say it in jest, I'll destroy anyone who has hurt her.

Ingrid sighs and pulls me tighter. "Fuck, I missed you."

"Never again. You have to know I won't be able to walk away from this," I speak into her hair, refusing to let go.

"You are, though. In a few short weeks, you'll be gone."

"Not exactly." She looks up, and as much as I want to claim her perfect lips, we need to talk about this. "They're finalizing my contract, but I'm part of a small unit that's been asked to come back. From the sound of it, I'm not going overseas. I'm supposed to have a call with them later this week to finalize arrangements. I won't be here, but we'll be able to talk every day, and I'll have time to come home often." Sure, it'll be a shitty two years, but I went ten without her. I'd give another ten if I had to.

"What if they do send you somewhere?"

"They won't." I lean in and kiss her forehead, holding her close.

"You know you basically sealed our fate that you're going to get called on some top-secret mission and will disappear off the face of the earth for a couple of years." Ingrid laughs and warms me in a way I can't explain. I'm still head-over-heels in love with her; I have to find a way to keep her. "Besides, you have quite the tall order before you leave. You promised you'd make me fall in love with you. People don't fall in love in three weeks, Cay."

"They do in your books."

"Like you'd know," she playfully scoffs.

I bend enough to reach behind her legs and pull them around me. "I do know."

Ingrid takes off my hat and puts it on. "You have the backward baseball cap thing down."

*Oh, my sweet, naive Ingrid. You have no idea.*

"Is that a thing?" I shrug. "I guess I didn't get to that part of the book."

I'm so full of shit. There's no specific scene I'm referring to, but I know *exactly* what's in her books. I haven't read anything on her ereader, but my sister has forced me to read a few romance novels, insisting it would help me find the perfect girl when I came back home.

I had already found the perfect girl and lost her, but this time I'm not going let her go. Second chance romance, perhaps? Based on the blush creeping up Ingrid's neck, I'm starting one of the books on her device as soon as we get home.

Looking out onto the water to make sure we're still alone, I bring us over to one of the built-in lounge chairs. As she slides her hands up my chest and around my neck, she stays a breath away from my lips, taunting me to make a move. Our lips barely brush, but I don't give in.

"Please." The moment her whispered beg passes her lips, I officially lose the upper hand, incapable of denying her. I need to touch her, taste her, claim her—I'm fucking desperate to hear her scream my name as I take her over the edge.

I slide my hands up her smooth thighs, gripping where they meet her hips. "How is it that all it takes is a 'please,' and I'm at your mercy?"

Ingrid wastes no time unfastening my pants, and I pull them down to my knees. Grinding her wet pussy against my length, I hiss as she whispers beside my ear, "As much as it was fun tying your hands, I think I prefer it the other way around."

I remove my hat from her head and toss it aside, letting her newly-dyed hair curtain our faces as it blows in the wind. I glide my hand in it and pull her back enough to drink her in; I want to memorize every inch of her.

A brief moment of stillness passes between us, but in an instant, her lips crash into mine, knocking me further back into the seat. I've had her sweet kisses, this is something else entirely. It's frenzied, messy, as if she can't get close enough, needing me as much as I need her. Reaching between us, I slip my cock inside her, and she exhales a sigh of wanting against my lips. I don't let her ride me; instead, I grip her hips, rocking her deeper onto my cock.

When she tries to pull up, I keep her close, kissing her jaw as I trail my lips down to her neck. "Let me take care of you."

Listening beautifully, I'm able to properly worship her. My hands move to her perfectly round ass, gently kneading as I continue at the same pace. This beautiful goddess on top of me will be the last woman I ever touch, but more importantly, the last I'll love. She's it for me. I'm lost in the moment of adoration, when she lifts up and slams back down onto my cock, pulling me back to reality.

"I thought I told you to let me take care of you." It comes out as a snarl, and she chuckles in response. "You think that's funny?" I graze my teeth against the spot I marked her and her soft laugh quickly becomes a moan. "Tell me what you need."

When she doesn't reply, I catalog my options. Being on the boat, there aren't many. She needs more, but I'm afraid of taking it too far. I can slide down the seat and have her ride my face, or let her continue… *and risk coming inside her.* After her confession this morning, we need to be safe.

I thrust up, pulling her completely onto me, and hold her there. "I don't have condoms."

"I'm on the shot. But if you want to stop…"

"I told you before to use me to come. You don't stop until you've made a mess all over my cock." I take a fistful of her hair, twisting it around my hand, and guide her lips to mine. She gives as much as she takes. I thought she wanted sweet and sensual. I was so wrong; my girl wants it fast and rough.

*So much for taking things slowly…*

Ingrid's lips never leave mine as she chases her orgasm. While it feels good, something isn't right—it isn't like this morning. Her pussy tightens, and just as I think she's close, she stops with my cock buried inside her.

"What's wrong?"

Her breath broken, she manages, "We can't do this."

"Hey," I say softly, taking her face in my hands and assuring her, "It's okay. I'm sorry."

"No." She shakes her head, placing a hand over mine and kissing my palm. "I'm sorry. I'm not going to use you."

I've been perpetually hard since the moment she came into town. The playing and teasing is going to have my cock revolting, even if it's my own fault. At least if she came, I could forgive myself for our first time and the missed years I should've had with her. My cock can forgive me when she's finally mine.

"Cay, I have to be honest with you." *Oh no.* "I never had an orgasm with anyone until you… this morning."

"What? No. There's no way. You're full of shit."

"Don't get me wrong. I come by myself all the time. But I can't use you to get off; you're not one of my toys. You're… you're *you*. Using you feels wrong," she sighs, swallowing a sob. "I can't lose you… I mean, *use* you."

My heart nearly leaps out of my chest at her admission. "Then don't. Let me love you the way I should have when we were younger. We can create a ridiculous list of things you want to do, in and out of bed, before I leave. But even when I do have to go"—I tuck her wind-swept hair behind her ear—"I'm always going to be yours."

"Can we do the thing I roll my eyes at in books?"

"What's that?" I laugh.

*"I can't believe I'm saying this*… Make love to me?"

I slide my hand to the front of her throat and pull her to me until our lips collide. Between kisses, I mutter, "We're in the middle of the lake. Let me take you home where I can properly show you how much you mean to me." Trailing with a feather-light touch down her body, I slip my hand under her dress and circle my thumb around her clit. "After you come."

"Cay…"

"Once. For me." I lift her off my shaft a few inches, and quickly pull down.

"Once," she whispers, her head falls back as she resumes riding me.

"Eyes on me, beautiful. I want to watch you fall apart." Ingrid's gaze snaps to mine for a moment, but it's too much for her. She leans in, our bodies flush, and I wrap my arm around her, guiding her further onto my cock as I thrust up inside her. Kissing her shoulder, her neck, every inch of skin I have access to, I whisper, "You're perfect, and you're mine, Ingrid." While she's giving me her body, I intend to steal her heart for myself, too. They aren't empty words, I just can't risk scaring her by admitting I'm still in love with her.

"Fuck, right there, I'm so close… Come with me?" Her moans and words vibrate against me. She feels too fucking good in my arms and wrapped around my cock, I'm moments away from coming. As I increase the pressure on her clit, it doesn't take long before she screams my name in pleasure. I'm addicted to the sound, already needing to hear my name from her lips again.

My lap is drenched as her pussy pulses around me. With a final thrust, I pull her impossibly closer and command, "One more. Give me one more."

I quicken my pace, and her body tenses. "I don't think I— *oh fuck*, that feels good…"

"You can do it. Give me one more, and I'll fill you." She's still coming down from her high when the second orgasm is in reach. "Just like that. Fuck, you're doing so well. Let go for me."

As her pussy tightens, pulsing around me, I can't hold on a moment longer. I come harder than I have in my life, my cock soaked with both of us. There will never be anyone after Ingrid. This is it, I'm fucking hers. Forever. Our breathing is erratic, and my cock twitches inside her as she takes every last drop. Wrapping her arms tighter around me, our hearts beat in sync.

We sit there for several minutes with my cock already hardening again, neither one of us saying a word. I don't want to take her again, especially since the silence is eerily similar to the first time we were together. This time, I savor having her in my arms, her face nuzzled in the crook of my neck, and the cool lake air whipping around us.

*She's mine.*

I reach below the seat into the storage compartment, pulling out a heavy flannel blanket and draping it over us. She sighs deeply, making no move to get up. Her breathing slows as she falls asleep on my chest.

The afternoon sun is dipping lower, shining brightly off the water. So much has happened since she arrived, never in a million years would I have guessed that I'd have her here with me, falling asleep on me with my cock still buried inside her. But no matter how much today has been everything I've ever wanted, I still have a dragon to slay for her.

# ingrid

...

"Hey, sweetheart, it's getting late," Caleb's deep voice rumbles beneath me.

"Ten more minutes," I murmur, settling closer against his warm, hard body. "Please?" He laughs, and the vibration tickles my cheek. I tilt my chin enough to press a soft kiss to his jaw, but my eyes fly wide as his cock twitches once inside me. "Cay!"

"Yeah?"

"You're still inside me…"

"So?"

"Cay!"

"Yes?"

*Fuck, this is gonna be gross when I get off you.*

He kisses my forehead, speaking against my skin, "We'll take a shower as soon as we get home."

"We are *not* making a habit of this…"

"But I like having you all to myself out here."

I carefully press against him, then lift off his cock and stand to the side of him. I offer my hand palm up expectantly, even though my focus is on my aching pussy. The emptiness is almost unbearable. "Where are my swimsuit bottoms?"

Caleb moves the blanket aside and reaches into his cargo shorts, retrieving the bottoms. "These?" As I grab at for them, he tosses them into the lake.

"Cay!"

"Have I told you how much I love when you scream my name?" My eyes narrow, my lips pursed. "I'll buy you new ones." Gripping the front of my dress, he pulls me onto him. "So much easier for me to taste you when you're not wearing them."

"I'll admit, that's a good line, but… please wait until after a shower?" I dismount again and pull his flannel shirt tighter around me.

Caleb looks off to where the sun is dangerously close to the mountain. "It'll have to wait, we have about twenty minutes to get back to the dock."

He stands and pulls up his boxer briefs and shorts, fastening them. Without a word, he takes my hand and practically drags me back to the steering wheel and sits me in the captain's chair, then raises the anchor. As he pulls it up, the muscles in his arms and back flex, his shirt straining to contain them. Once it's in the boat, he grabs a large pole and fishes my swimsuit bottoms from the water and tosses it onto the deck. He looks back at me, accepting his small defeat—I should've known that he never would've left them there.

Stepping behind me, he starts the engine and shifts the gear, then places my hands on the wheel. "I'm not driving this thing, Cay."

"Yes, you are." After a moment of me steering us around the bend and into view of the dock, he kisses my neck and whispers, "I'll help you when we get closer, but you've got this." I keep my hands firmly planted at ten and two, feeling like I'm in high school, moments away from failing my driving test. "Keep it steady, I'm going to increase the speed." He shifts the gear again then places his hand on my thigh. "Just like that."

Caleb slides his hand up my dress, but I clench my legs together. "Really? I'm going to crash your boat, and we'll become fish food."

"I'd never let you crash," he chuckles, moving his hand lower and pulls his hand from my dress. Keeping it on top of the fabric, he splays his hand on my stomach. "I've always been yours, Ingrid. You have to tell me if something is too much or not enough. It'll never change how I feel about you if you tell me to stop."

*Fuck, I don't deserve him.*

A few moments pass and he slows down the boat. "Are you going to take over? I don't know how to properly pull into the dock."

"You don't need me to do it for you. I'll walk you through it." His voice is steady, reassuring, even if I'm ninety percent sure I'm going to ram the dock with his boat and have to file a really weird insurance claim.

*Hi, yes, my crush from high school was trying to be sweet, but he seduced me while I parked this party boat. Is that covered as an "at-fault" accident or…?*

Caleb slows the boat to a stop, then pulls out what looks like giant inflatables and attaches them to the sides. He looks up and explains. "I'm putting bumpers up."

"Is this like bowling? You're putting up the little rails for five-year-olds to make sure I don't gutter-ball?"

He lets out a full laugh and opens two of the doors of the boat, then makes his way back to me. "Yeah, basically." He steps behind me again, and instead of maintaining a steady speed, he's doing little bumpy bumps on the gear shift. "We're going to glide in at a thirty degree angle. When we get close, turn the wheel all the way toward the dock. It's going to swing the boat where we want it. Then, when we're about ten feet out, you're going to turn it all the way to the left, since that's where we're docking."

"What the fuck, Cay? I don't know what any of that means!"

"I'm right here, I won't let you crash."

He walks me through the steps again, and once we are right up to the dock, he hops out and helps to guide us into what's essentially a parking spot for his boat. Grabbing the rope from the boat, he ties it to one of the dock anchors, but a wave pulls the back of the boat away from the dock.

"Cay!" I check, and he's already turned off the motor, so I'm not sure what to do.

Caleb hops into the pontoon and rushes to me, taking me in his arms. "You did so good. It's ok." His arms are freezing, so I begin taking off his flannel, but he stops me and growls, "Absolutely not."

"You're cold, and—"

"I'm going to tie off the boat, stay here." He kisses my temple and releases me to finish. He starts the motor for a moment, steers the wheel, and we become flush with the dock. Once everything is shut down, he hops out again and ties the back of the boat to the dock. "All right, princess, let's get you home."

# caleb

### . . .

I've spent the past four days feeling like I'm living in some sort of dream sequence. With the clock ticking, every moment I'm not working or helping Pop, I'm spending time with Ingrid or taking her out for proper dates—*and improper dates*. Each night, we're either at her place or mine, as it always should've been.

No. It should've been *our* place.

Sitting at the bar, waiting for me to finish work, she gasps, "Cay, I've made the shortlist!"

I finish pouring a pint for Tim and rush over to her. "Shortlist for what?"

"A Silver Globe." She looks up from her phone. "I might get nominated this year for 'Writing—Comedy Series.'"

Immediately, a smile splits my face. "No, you're not just going to be nominated, you're going to fucking win it, princess." Her eyes narrow at the name that I can't seem to stop using. "You know I'll buy you the biggest fucking tiara for the ceremony."

"Don't get ahead of yourself, I haven't even been nominated, yet," she laughs, but it ceases quickly. There's too much publicity around her at the moment. I try my best to ignore the news articles, but some of it is unavoidable when the notifications hit my phone. Yesterday, she had to get a new number because her phone wouldn't stop ringing with media inquiries. Her agent seems to be fucking worthless. A few ruthless reporters even came to town, but Ashlyn and the rest of the sheriff's department have helped ensure that people who don't belong here stay far away from my girl.

I round the bar and swivel Ingrid in her seat. "You're going to be nominated, and you're going to win." Cupping her neck, I kiss her forehead, and she leans into my touch —which I've discovered I both love and hate. I only have two weeks with her before I leave, and each time I kiss her is one closer to being our last.

A familiar throat clears to the side of me and I groan, "Hey, Cass."

"Who is winning what?"

"Ingrid is going to win an award for writing," I answer before Ingrid can try to diminish the good news.

"That's amazing! I'm off for the night, want to hang out?" Cassidy sits on the other side of Ingrid. "Movie night?"

"I'll watch a movie with you," Travis chimes in, taking a seat next to Cassidy. "Or make one."

She rolls her eyes and pivots her seat to tell Ingrid, "Girls' night?"

"Oh, I was going to have dinner with Cay when he's off—"

"Go," I whisper beside Ingrid's ear. "I know you want to. Text me when you're done, and I'll pick you up."

"A girls' night would be great," Ingrid corrects, bringing a beaming smile to my sister's face. "What movie do you have in mind?"

While the girls talk, I get back to work and grab Travis a drink. Hand poised to pour his usual IPA from the tap, but he stops me. "Just water." The entire bar goes silent, all eyes on him.

The last time a firefighter came into the bar and ordered water was after a massive fire a few towns over where a few people didn't make it. I wasn't here when it happened, but from what I've heard, it's been a tradition ever since.

"Everything ok?" I ask quietly.

"We, uh"—he removes his cap and rakes his hand through his sandy-blond hair—"we lost one today."

I heard there was a fire in Crest Canyon, but it seemed contained. I pour a water and place it in front of Travis. Cassidy gets up from her seat and joins me on my side of the bar. She takes out a pint glass and fills it with water. She clinks the glass with him and drinks it. With a lopsided smile, Travis huffs a small laugh. "Thanks."

It's then that I look around at the rest of the patrons and, without thinking, pull out as many clean pint glasses as I can find and fill each one about a third full with water. Cassidy and Ingrid pass them out to everyone. Cassidy raises her newly-filled pint and awaits Travis' toast.

Travis stands and raises his glass. "We lost Blaze today." The entire bar gasps. "He was a good pup. Saved a little girl today. We'll miss him always." Travis' voice cracks at the end; no one would dare ask him to continue.

"To Blaze," Cassidy shouts, and the rest of the bar echoes, "To Blaze."

Once the fervor dies down, Travis asks me, "Are you busy with the misses tomorrow morning?"

I glance at Ingrid who is talking to Cassidy, then back to Travis. "Depends. How early?"

# ingrid

· · ·

S pending the night without Caleb was strange, but definitely needed. Things are getting too comfortable. In a couple of short weeks I won't be waking up next to him, or with his face between my legs—it'll be cold sheets next to me, and if I'm lucky, a call once every few days. When Cass offered for me to stay the night, it was the perfect excuse to put a little space between Caleb and me.

Sitting on her couch with a mug of coffee, I'm doom scrolling social media while I wait for Cass to wake up, and an email pings my inbox that stands out among all the media inquiries.

---

To: ingrid@ingridlawrence.com
CC: devon@fateagency.com
From: tsmith@romanceflix.com
Subject: RE: Head Writer Query for Maybe in Fifty

Irene Bahrd

Ms. Lawrence,

Thank you for your interest.

While we recently acquired the rights for the title, it includes provisions by the book's author, Ms. Amanda Black, to appoint the writing staff.

We have forwarded your information to her and will reach out within the next few weeks to discuss the next steps, should it be the right fit.

Regards,

Timothy Smith
Human Resources
Romance Flix, Inc

---

While I don't love the idea of switching from primetime to a streaming service, I adore the author's books, and it would be a dream come true to work on the script for the mini-series. For the first time in a week, everything feels like it's falling into place. It's only a matter of time before the chatter dies down about how I left the network, so between this glimmer of hope and the potential that I'll be nominated for an award…

*If only Caleb wasn't leaving.*

"You're up early," Cass grumbles, plopping herself on the couch next to me. She takes my coffee from me and finishes it in four quick gulps. "Need another?"

"No," I laugh, "but guess what?"

"You're moving in?" She stands to make herself another cup.

"No, but maybe the opposite," I reply meekly.

"You're moving in with Cay?"

"No! I've been back a week, I'm sure as hell not moving in with him. I got an email from Romance Flix; they've sent my information to the book's author. I've heard from other writers that she's a control freak and always picks her own team for her movies and mini-series projects. The fact that they emailed me back... I have a good feeling about it."

"Look at you, Miss I'm Going Places." While she's teasing, her tone is still full of pride. "That's fucking amazing. So, how much longer before you leave for another decade?"

"*Cass...*"

"I'm kidding! Okay, I'm not. What about Caleb? Does he know?"

I shake my head. "No, I just got the email. There's no point in saying anything, I haven't been offered the job. Who knows where they will want me to be to write it, but he's leaving in a couple of weeks anyway."

Once her coffee is poured, she sits on the couch and faces me. "You know I love you; you're family. But Cay? He's been obsessed with you since we were kids. I think in his mind, he's going to leave for two years and come back home to find you waiting on his porch or something. Don't get me wrong, that's on him, but I don't see you staying here, even if they let you write remotely."

"I know," I sigh. "I love being home. It's quiet, things are slower…"

"But?"

"But, I miss the city! I miss being able to grab a slice of pizza at two in the morning. I miss the hustle and bustle. I miss being able to walk through Central Park when I need to clear my head. I…" *But I'll miss Caleb when he's gone, more.*

"What?"

I shake away the thought. "Nothing. I just miss my life." Taking her hand in mine, I add, "You can come with me?"

"To visit? Sure. But I'd never survive in the concrete jungle. I love my life here. I know I joke about you two running off into the sunset, but things are getting serious between you and Cay. I just hope you're both being careful."

"We're not," I wince. "This is weird to talk about with you, but I don't know that I can handle having someone in my life who is basically a temporary boyfriend. We have an expiration date. Who in their right mind starts a relationship knowing it's going to end?"

"I think that's where you're wrong. I don't think he sees it ending. It's not some summer fling for him." Her phone vibrates, and she checks it. "Speak of the devil… *Aww.*" She shows me her text messages.

CALEB

Meet Inferno.

It's accompanied by a picture of Travis snuggling a Dalmatian, and I burst out in laughter. I was so worried that Caleb would send a hot photo of him with a puppy, but turns out Cass is getting all the thirst traps. A moment later, my own phone dings with a message from Caleb.

Just say yes.

To what?

The next text is a photo of him holding an adorable Dalmatian puppy. I'm not sure who is cuter, though: him cuddling with a dog, or the sweet pup itself.

No.

But she's beautiful.

You're leaving in two weeks.

I'm bringing her home.

Who is going to take care of her?

Travis said he'll help watch her until I get back.

He'll share custody with you, of course.

What do you want to name her?

You can name your dog whatever you want.

Our dog.

"Well, it looks like your brother has adopted a dog..." I show her the texts, and she coughs a laugh. "This isn't funny."

"It totally is, and you should name her *Smitten*."

# caleb

. . .

I pull up to Cass' place and click the leash onto the collar of Ingrid's and my new addition. She leaps out of the truck with me, and I make sure she empties her bladder before we knock on the door.

Travis wasn't trying to replace Blaze. He wanted a dog of his own that he wouldn't have to share with the boys at the station. When he met Inferno, it was love at first sight, and when Inferno's sweet little sister curled up into my lap, I fell in love with my own little pup. I wasn't teasing when I told Ingrid that she's our dog, and I selfishly want something to tie us together when I'm gone. I know they're a lot of work. So, when Travis offered to help if Ingrid needed it, I couldn't say no to these adorable brown eyes, and had to bring her home.

Cassidy opens the door and gasps, "You really got her." She crouches down and pets her behind the ear, calling into the house, "Smitten's here!"

"We are not calling her Smitten," Ingrid insists, coming up behind Cass. "Fuck, Cay, what were you thinking?"

"Smitten is perfect. Isn't she pretty?" Cass coos. "Who's a good dog? You are."

"She's beautiful, but she's going to be huge!" Ingrid crosses her arms over her chest.

"I'll take her to the backyard; she's not potty trained yet." I move past my sister and Ingrid to take the pup out back. She shouldn't have an accident, but I know once Ingrid sees her jumping around in the backyard, she'll fall in love just like I did.

With each step, the weight of my actions hits me. It was reckless to adopt a dog before I leave, especially if the unthinkable happens and Ingrid and I aren't together. I quickly squash the idea—we aren't going to end, she's my forever.

Once on the back porch, I take off the leash and let Smitten roam. Cass and Ingrid join me moments later and Cass whispers, "If Ingrid doesn't want her, I do," making me chuckle.

"What happens when you leave?" Ingrid asks, watching our pup leap through the overgrown grass.

"She'll have you, Travis, and Cass." I shrug. "I can't have her on base, but the minute I'm home, she'll stay with us."

Ingrid chews on her lip. "What if I'm not here?"

A slap wouldn't have stung as much. "What are you talking about?"

Cass whips her head in Ingrid's direction, then looks at me with wide eyes. "I, uh… I'm going to take Smitten for a walk. Show her the neighborhood." Cass takes the leash from me and pats her lap. Even though the pup isn't fully trained, she comes in an instant. She stops in front of Ingrid and sits. "Well, that's bullshit."

Ingrid drops to her knees and pets her. "Smitten suits you, little one." I hadn't thought of any names, but if Ingrid likes it, it works for me. Ingrid sighs, and Smitten nuzzles her hand. Cass waits a few moments while Ingrid bonds with our little pup. When Ingrid finally looks up, a small smirk tries to escape as she insists, "If she's staying with you, we need to go buy everything she needs." I drop to a knee and take Ingrid's chin between my thumb and fore-finger, bringing her lips to mine. "Don't think you can just kiss me and pretend you didn't just adopt a dog this morning."

"Okay, on that note…" Cass leashes up Smitten and heads into the house, to take her for a walk. "Oh, and please don't fuck in my house. I'll be back in a bit. Call me if you need something."

Cass leaves, and Ingrid and I drive over to my place to spend the afternoon prepping my house for Smitten. I feel as if I'm baby-proofing a home; putting up gates, ensuring cabinets aren't accessible and electrical cords are out of reach. We also bought a large dog bed, the best quality food we can purchase in town, and more toys than Smitten will know what to do with. Admittedly, it's as if I'm playing house with Ingrid, and I can't help feeling a pang of hurt knowing there a small chance we could've been doing something similar when we were younger.

We'd have an almost ten-year-old now, and my life would've taken on a very different trajectory.

While putting up the last gate, Ingrid asks, "What am I supposed to do when you're gone and I move?" I'm so caught up in everything that Ingrid's question feels like it comes out of nowhere.

"Do you want to move in here while I'm gone?" I ask hopefully.

"No," she answers without a hint of hesitation. "This morning, I got an email back from a production company. I might be interviewing for a head writing position for a series. I know the author of the book they are adapting lives in Scotland, but I don't think they'll send me there. It'll probably be filmed in Los Angeles or New York. Maybe Canada. I might have to move. If not this job, maybe another one. I can bring Smitten with me but"—she shakes her head, shutting her eyes—"this is moving too fast."

All at once, I know I'm losing her. "What are you saying?"

"Cay, I've been in town for a week. One week and you're adopting dogs, and basically asking me to move in. You have to see how crazy that is." She takes a deep breath, and my stomach drops. "I'll take the blame for being swept up in the fantasy, but the reality is in a few short weeks, you're gone."

"Only for two years, and if I can't call, I'll write you every day."

"Please don't," she snaps. "It'll only make things harder."

I take a step closer, but she takes one back to keep her distance. "Ingrid…"

"I'm sorry, I just need some time to think, so I'm going to stay at my place tonight. Cass mentioned coming by in about an hour with Smitten. If you need help, I'll come by, but if I stay the night, I'm going to sleep on the couch." Just as I think she's going to leave, she wraps her arms around my middle. "I don't want to end things, but I just need everything to slow down for us to figure it out."

I hold her tighter and kiss the top of her head. The clock is still ticking, and I'm still leaving. She was right the first night I spent with her: One of us will get hurt. We do need to slow things down; I'm not going to lose her because of this. "Maybe a clean break is the best? We can pick up where we left off when I come home."

"Why does it have to be all or nothing?"

"You're my everything, Ingrid, it'll never be nothing,"

"So, now what? We don't see each other or talk until you're back?"

I blow out a long breath but won't let go of her until I absolutely have to. "You deserve better than two weeks. Hell, we both do. I don't know where the answer lies, but I refuse to accept that this is the end."

"'Clean break' sounds a hell of a lot like the end, Cay," she whispers, angling her chin and looking up at me.

"What do you want?" I risk asking, unsure if I even want the answer.

Her eyes search mine. "I don't know. Just not what we're doing."

"Stay with me tonight. I'll see if Cass can watch the pup, and we can spend one last night, just you and me. In the morning, we'll set the two-year timer. I just want to wake up next to you if I have to wait years to do it again."

It'll be torture. She should deny me and save us both the heartbreak. Instead, she whispers, "Okay," and lifts onto her toes to kiss me gently. She's being careful, and I let her.

I bend to pull her legs up and around my waist, then lead us into the kitchen and set her on the counter. I stand between her thighs and glide my fingers into her hair, resting my thumb on her cheek. As I close the distance, I stop with our lips a mere whisper apart when my phone buzzes in my pocket. I sigh, and reluctantly check it, finding an unknown number calling. Sending it to voicemail, I mutter, "Fucking spam," but then send a quick text asking Cass if she can take Smitten tonight. I don't wait for her reply and toss the phone on the counter. "Where was I?"

Ingrid smiles, and it's one that reaches her eyes. I know this is the stupidest idea I've ever come up with—one night with her will never be enough. I could never ask for her to wait for me, but I pray she will all the same. I capture her mouth with mine, desperate to take advantage of every last moment I have with her. If tonight is all I get, I'll make sure it's the longest fucking night in existence.

*And have her aching for a second.*

When I'm gone, I want to be the first thing she thinks about when she wakes up each morning, and selfishly, I want her hand between her legs each night, counting down the days until I'm back and buried inside her.

Gripping her ass and pulling her body flush with mine, I'm lost in the taste of her sweet mouth when the phone ringing has my entire world crashing down around me. *No. Fuck!* My landline number is unlisted—only Pop and the Navy have it.

"Fuck," I groan, reluctantly pulling back from Ingrid.

"What's wrong?"

I cross the kitchen and answer it, my heart beating out of my chest. "Rogers."

"Commander Caleb Rogers?"

"Yes, Sir."

"This is Admiral Beckett. Code word?"

"Daffodil."

"Please confirm your line is secure."

I pull up the data on the phone to confirm no one is listening in and mute the call. "Ingrid, don't say a word, okay?" She nods, and I unmute the phone. "Line is secure."

"Commander Rogers, we'll need to bring you in early."

*No.*

"How early?"

"A car will be at your home at 0400 tomorrow morning. Please make sure you have any essential medications, identification, your blues and your whites. Do you have any additional questions?"

"No, Sir."

"Thank you for your service." The line goes dead.

*This can't be fucking happening…*

"What's going on?" Ingrid asks carefully.

"Remember when you joked that I jinxed myself?"

She frowns. "No."

"Do I still get one night?"

"What's going on, Cay?"

"Do I still get one night?" I repeat, this time it comes out rougher than I thought it would, making Ingrid's eyes fill with worry. I take a deep breath. "I'm leaving in the morning."

"What?" She hops off the counter. "You have two weeks."

"No. I don't know what's going on, but they wouldn't be calling me in unless it was an international incident or there's something wrong with a sub. I don't want to think the worst, but… I need to know you'll be safe when I'm gone."

"Of course I'll be safe," she scoffs, but she must see the worry in my features when she repeats matter-of-factly, "I'll be safe."

"I have to see Pop and Cass before I go, but… Please stay with me tonight? I understand if you don't want to. This isn't like we're easing out of this like we planned. I have to leave, and I have no fucking clue where I'm going or when I'll be able to talk to you again." She looks away as if she's trying to figure out another way out of this. "Please, Ingrid. I won't touch you, I just—"

"Go see your dad and Cass, I'll be here when you get back."

I trace her jaw with my thumb and press a single kiss to her lips. "I'll be back before you know it."

# ingrid

. . .

After the whirlwind of today, I'm exhausted, pacing after waiting over three hours for Caleb. I slide under the covers of his perfectly made bed and try to calm my mind. So much has happened in so little time. I grab my ereader that he insisted on keeping until he leaves, and since it's dead, I'm left with just my phone to pass the time. Unfortunately, it's down to the last ten percent of the battery, so I plug both of them in to charge the devices.

Closing my eyes, I take long, deep breaths, taking in the scent of him on the pillows. It's a mix of his cologne, fabric softener, and everything I've come to know as *him*. I'm going to miss waking up next to Cay when he's gone.

*Maybe I was too harsh about all of it?*

*No, he got a dog for us…*

My eyes become heavier, and sleep overtakes me. I've never been much of a dreamer, but tonight, I'm having vivid dreams of being tied up by Caleb as he worships every inch of me. As I'm about to come in my dream, I'm jolted awake by a hand splayed on my stomach, pulling my back against a hard chest.

"Shh, it's just me. I'm sorry I woke you," Caleb murmurs as he kisses my shoulder.

Still turned on by my dream, I'm torn between wanting him to touch me, and just enjoying being in his arms. We need to talk about things, but with him leaving, maybe it's all left better unsaid. I'm grateful he decides for us, wrapping his strong arms around me and kissing every inch of bare skin he has access to, not pushing for more. I turn in his embrace, and our legs intertwine. Comfortably wrapped up with him, I fall back asleep.

A few hours later, my breath is uneven, and my eyes flutter open. Heat pools in my belly and I have an overwhelming desperation to come. I grip the sheets beneath me as Caleb's tongue expertly circles my clit.

"Sorry, princess, I needed one last taste," he whispers, slipping two fingers inside me.

"Please," the only word that passes my lips.

I lift my hips to take them deeper and grind against his mouth, needing more. He curls inside me and sucks hard on my clit. It's almost enough, I'm teetering on the edge.

"Right there, please. Don't stop."

Caleb chuckles against me, and the vibration is fucking delicious against my clit. After only a few minutes, my body is simultaneously shivering and on fire as my orgasm tears through me. He doesn't let up, sucking harder as I nearly black out.

I loosen my grip on the sheets and my heart rate begins to steady. "Cay," I breathe, barely a whisper.

He kisses up my body until his lips reach mine. I wrap my legs around him, pressing my bare pussy against his hard cock, soaking his boxer briefs. As his tongue sweeps across mine, he's in no hurry, tasting me as if he's trying to commit the moment to memory.

Trailing his kisses down to my neck, he draws my skin into his mouth and sucks hard, making me gasp. I tangle my hand in his hair and press him closer as he marks me— with him leaving, I want it to last weeks. His lips drag up to mine for a long, languid kiss that makes my toes curl. I whimper a sigh when we break apart, and he then rests his forehead on mine for a moment before sliding to the side of me. Gripping my hip, he turns me onto my side and wraps his strong arms around me, his wall of a chest pressed against my back.

It's not enough, I'm desperate to get closer. Reaching behind me, I try to slip his boxer briefs down, but he swats my hand away. "I need you," I beg, coming out as a strangled whisper.

Caleb doesn't reply, only kisses the mark he left. Sliding his hand lower, he pulls my thighs apart and slips his fingers inside me while he cups my breast with his free hand. Everything is simultaneously too much and not enough. My heart aches, knowing this may be the last time he'll touch me in… *Who knows how long?*

With Caleb's cock pressed against my ass, I can't help my whine, wishing he was inside me. He doesn't give in, continuing to massage his fingers, kissing my shoulder. It's sweet and loving, but it only makes all of this hurt more.

I turn in his arms and press him onto the mattress to straddle him. He doesn't fight me, sliding his hands up and down my thighs, a swirl of pain and pleasure dancing in his eyes. "What do you need?"

"You, Cay. I need you."

He grips the front of my throat and pulls me to him as my lips crash into his. "Hands on the headboard, princess." I do as he asks and he slides further between my legs until my pussy is hovering over his mouth. Without warning, he grips my ass and forces me to sit on his face. His tongue dives into me, curls once, then drags up to my clit, sucking hard. A loud groan rumbles beneath me.

Licking firm but lazy circles, he teases the hell out of me. I roll my hips seeking more, but he refuses. I need to come… but my need for him is more. And he fucking knows it.

I can't explain it or rationalize it. Of course we moved fast. He's everything I've ever wanted, what I was missing all these years. In this moment, I want to take it all back, let us fall hard and risk being heartbroken for years. He's leaving in the morning, and I….

*Fuck. I love him.*

All at once, my second orgasm overtakes me. "*Cay!*" Every nerve ending is on fire. My head falls back, and I nearly lose my hold on the headboard.

My body buzzing, he slides out from under me. I know in my soul that this is the last man I'm ever going to sleep with. The thought no longer scares me, but I don't want to risk making things harder by voicing it aloud. As I catch my breath, Caleb snakes his arm around my waist, and I fall back against him. "You're going to give me one more." His tone doesn't have the same command it normally has. The angst in his voice breaks my heart in two; we both know this is the last time he'll touch me for the foreseeable future.

Caleb pulls down his boxer briefs, then pushes his cock inside me with ease. I savor every thrust as he spends the next couple of hours buried inside me, worshiping each other's bodies.

He was always mine, but now… I'm his.

Deliciously sore and exhausted, he kisses my forehead, and though his voice is faint, I still hear him whisper, "I love you, Ingrid. I'll always love you." It's the last thing I hear as I drift off to sleep.

---

The sun peeks through the curtains, making me shut my eyes tightly and pull a pillow over my head. "Cay, can you close the drapes?" When he doesn't answer, I reach for him, met with cool sheets where he should be next to me. "No. *No, no, no.*" I abruptly sit up and look around the room. "Cay?" I call out, praying he's in the kitchen making coffee. I check the time. 8:43. "Fuck!"

*This has to be a dream… He's not leaving, we just had a little argument, and he'll walk in any minute now with coffee in hand and a pretty Dalmatian waltzing in behind him.*

I scramble out of bed, my sore pussy my first clue that I didn't dream it. Glancing down I find I'm bottomless but wearing my tee from yesterday, confirming it all happened.

I shut my eyes as his whispered words echo in my mind. *"I love you, Ingrid."*

"I love you, too," I say quietly into the empty room.

I check the bedside tables… Only my phone is plugged in.

The dresser… His jeans and tees are still neatly folded.

The closet… His dress blues and whites are missing.

A cold chill cascades down my limbs, and I remain rooted in place. He's gone; it wasn't a dream. I was upset about how everything was moving too fast, but now it feels as if maybe we moved too slowly. I didn't even get to say goodbye.

I know nothing about what he did in the years he served in Navy, only what he told me about repairing submarines. Some of it was classified. My mind is cluttered with questions, and I don't know where to start.

*His dad is a retired naval officer…*

I put on underwear and leggings, grab my phone, and rush out of the bedroom into the kitchen to retrieve my purse. A piece of paper next to the coffee maker catches my attention.

*This isn't goodbye. I'll always be yours. You're my everything.*
*I love you.*

## Caleb

My heart squeezes. He might be my forever, too, but we didn't even have a chance to find out. Like idiots, we jumped in with two feet, and one week with him felt like a whole year.

I fold up the note and put it in my purse. As I make my way to the front door, I check my phone. About to text Cass, I find a missed call and voicemail from an unknown number. I click play and put it to my ear, sucking in a breath when I hear Caleb's voice.

*"Hey, princess. I'm about to get on the plane and don't know when or if I'll be able to call you again. No matter what happens, I need you to know that I'm going to do everything I can to return to you. When I'm back, I promise we won't move too fast. We'll date for fifteen years before I ask you to move in if you want. But, we both know it's supposed to be you and me in the end. I love you, Ingrid. I always will."*

It hurts to hear, but he's wrong. It wouldn't take fifteen years, I fell in love with him in a single week. Or a decade and a half, but who's counting? And now he's gone. It wouldn't matter if we hadn't fought, or whatever the hell that was last night; he would've left this morning. I take solace in the fact that he didn't leave *me*, he left because he had to.

In one stupid week, my entire life has been turned upside down, and I feel emptier than I have in my whole life. I send a quick text to Cassidy that I'm going to go see her father, and come by for her and Smitten afterward. If anyone can help me through this, it's them.

# caleb

. . .

W e absolutely moved too fast. Ingrid didn't come home to Sapphire Lake for me, she was running from everything. Instead of letting her heal from whatever happened in New York, I ended up pushing her away.

We'll have to start over when I'm back. It's the only way I'll be able to keep her—if she'll still have me.

Though the commercial flight is short, I pull out Ingrid's ereader, hoping to read a chapter or two before I'm told to stow electronics. Picking up where I left off with the hockey romance I stealthily started this week, my seat-mate, Daniels, pulls my attention from it when he laughs, "Didn't take you for a romance reader?" I shift in my seat and continue reading, ignoring him. Unfortunately, he doesn't take the hint. "You'll need to switch over to your NeRD when we get on the ship, you know. Doubt they have that one loaded on there, though."

The ereaders they give us have mostly mysteries and fantasy books preloaded, so we can read at sea without the internet or disrupting any signals. It definitely won't have Ingrid's books downloaded. But to imply I'll need my NeRD isn't lost on me—it means they're putting me on a boat. "Have they briefed you?"

"No, but there's only one reason they'd call us, right?"

I can only hope wherever they are sending me will be quick so I can finish out my time and get back to Ingrid. I was supposed to be stationed in California with occasional travel; I negotiated for two years to assist with training teams for emergency repairs. With several countries across the Pacific putting boats in the water, there's the concern that we need more engineers on board to troubleshoot if they get hit.

I pull out my NeRD to see if there are any titles that match Ingrid's. I'm not surprised, there are none. As I let out a defeated sigh, Daniels chimes in, "Want me to add them?"

My eyes snap to him. "You can do that?"

A devilish smile appears, and he offers his hand expectantly. I give him the devices and he plugs in a wire into both. He swipes and clicks until it hits me that he's essentially pirating the titles.

"Stop." I cover my hand on one of the screens. "They aren't my books." He frowns. "They're my… wife's." Though it's a lie, it's easier than explaining she's the woman I'm planning on spending the rest of my life with. His expression doesn't change. "This is basically book piracy."

Daniels laughs, "I mean, technically. Tell you what, we can order all the same books in paperback and send them to the Mrs. That way you can read it without a guilty conscience."

It's one of the better ideas I've heard in the past twenty-four hours, though I still feel wrong about it. I pull out my phone that's still in airplane mode and click to access the in-flight Wi-Fi. Daniels works quickly to download as many of the books onto my NeRD as space will allow, while I order the books to be mailed to my house, on top of ebooks to be downloaded from my personal account when I'm home.

After talking with Pop last night, I practically begged him to convince Ingrid to move into my place while I'm gone, at least until she gets hired somewhere. She should have a pleasant surprise in a few days, though my conscience still gnaws at me.

"There, all set." He hands me the devices back and, sure enough, all of the titles I flagged are transferred over. While my NeRD doesn't have space for all of them, hope-fully, it will hold me over until I get back from wherever they are sending us.

"Thanks," I sigh. At least now I'll have one small connection to Ingrid while I'm gone.

"No problem! My girlfriend got me hooked on a fantasy series that wasn't available. I had to make sure I had a way to read them while we're gone. Last thing I want is to come home to is her spoiling the ending of book seven. Don't worry, I bought all of the special editions for my girl… Okay, fine, they were for me. But it's bullshit that they only give us shitty titles to download!"

"You know it's still wrong… right?"

"Oh, I'm going straight to hell for this," he laughs. "I suppose you will, too."

*Best to download the audiobooks for Ingrid, for good measure. Not spending my afterlife without her due to military logistical issues.*

Once we land, Daniels and I make quick work to text everyone before our phones are confiscated. Unfortunately, neither of us is fast enough when an officer with enough medals to set off a TSA detector from a mile away greets us. "Rogers. Daniels." We salute and he reaches his hand out, palm face up. "Phones, tablets, and laptops."

*Here we go…*

# ingrid

...

I rap my knuckles on David's door. It feels weird calling him David, but weirder calling him Mr. Rogers. He's always been Pop, but I don't deserve to call him that after everything that's happened.

There are hushed whispers before he opens the door. The scowl on his face quickly dissipates as soon as he sees me, replaced with worry painting his features. "Ingrid. Is everything ok?"

"I'm sorry, did I come at a bad time?" I glance around him, in search of the other voice I heard.

He follows my gaze, looking behind him into the house. "Oh, uh... Nope. Was just watching a movie."

When he turns back, I blurt, "Caleb's gone," the admission making tears prick behind my eyes. Choking them back, I repeat quietly, "Cay's... *gone*."

"I know, sweetheart," he sighs. "Do you want to come in?"

As I nod, he opens the door wider for me to enter. I make my way to the living room where the TV isn't on, but it's the least of my worries. Taking a seat on the sofa, he joins me.

Unable to handle the awkward situation, I break the silence. "I have some questions."

"What about?"

"Everything you know about the Navy."

He chuckles softly, "Well, I can't share anything classified. But what's on your mind?"

"There's a phone in his house. A landline. No one has landlines, except people in their seventies. He got a call last night, and he wasn't the sweet and fun Caleb I know. It was like he was a different man altogether. While on the call, he was serious, emotionless…"

"He's a specialist, he could get a call at any moment if there is an emergency. I can't get into specifics, but he was going back in for two years to train teams of people to prepare for those sorts of emergencies. The call he got wasn't part of that contract, he could be sent anywhere in the world. It could be one week or eight months."

"So, it was an emergency? Is he okay?"

"It's above my clearance, but you don't get that call if it's not serious. I tried to look into it, but I'm not able to access where he's headed or for how long." After a moment, he continues, "You know, my wife, Mary, hated when I would get the call. I had a duty to uphold, so I would leave without hesitation. When cancer took her from us, I retired. I couldn't have my kids worrying about me, or worse, risk orphaning them. It wasn't until Caleb followed in my footsteps that I really understood the fear she felt. He'll understand when he has a wife and kids of his own."

My breath catches, and my heart skips a beat. The idea of Caleb being with someone else is too unbearable a thought, but I don't know that I could handle living in constant fear.

"So, we just wait by the phone? Hope he's ok?"

"No," he laughs, "I know you've been gone for years, but I watched you grow up. You *never* waited for anything to happen, you *made* things happen. I'll always love you like you're one of my own, no matter what. Ingrid, you were meant to take on the world, not watch the world happen around you while you wait for a man, who could be on the other side of it."

I take in his words. Waiting for Caleb, I would feel stifled. Not waiting, I'll feel like a piece is missing.

"Did he tell you he adopted a dog?" I chuckle. "Said it's *our* dog."

"Oh, I heard." He smiles and shakes his head. "You've probably figured it out already, but he's only ever had eyes for you. I tried to warn him when you came back to take his time, but there's no stopping him when he sets his mind to something. He's stubborn, doesn't give up—part of why he's so good at his job, and why they called him." With a quick rake of his hair, he assures me, "Cass didn't tell me the details about why you're here, but there are only a handful of reasons you'd be back. None that come to mind are positive. But no matter what it was, I don't think it would've mattered to him."

"I do care about him," I sigh, unable to tell him the whole truth. "A lot. But, I came back because I needed Cass. Caleb and I were… unexpected. So, what do I do now?"

"Only you know the answer to that."

I chew on my lip. "What would *you* do?"

"It doesn't matter what I would do. You're not like Caleb —he can be a bit impulsive if you haven't noticed. You aren't. But, just like Cay, you've always had big plans and followed through on them. Caleb would wait a hundred years on his front porch if I told him you would show up one day. But you? You can wait by the phone *and* live your life at the same time if that's what you want to do. When I was away from Mary, I wrote to her every day in a journal. It might be good to do the same to tell him how you're feeling—even if angry—while he's away."

"And if he doesn't call?" My stomach twists, and my tears threaten to fall.

"I can't tell you how I know." He places his hand over mine. "But, he'll call you before he calls me."

We share a smile, and he pats my hand once before he stands. I join him and wrap my arms around his middle. "Thank you, David."

"Hey, now, none of that!" He releases me with a long sigh. "Being a Navy wife may or may not be in your future, but you'll always be a second daughter to me, no matter what happens with Caleb." I nod, and he leads me to the front door. As I walk out, he adds, "You can stay at Cay's or your place as long as you want. Just let me know if you need help moving your things."

"I think I'll stay at Cay's if that's okay? At least until I get a new job."

"I'll have everything moved over later today."

"Oh, you don't ha—"

"I insist."

With a final hug goodbye, I leave and climb into Caleb's truck to head over to Cassidy's. On the drive over, I mull everything over that's happened since I arrived. I asked Caleb to break my heart, and he asked me to break his. In a week, we managed to accomplish both. He was so quiet last night, I'm used to him telling me how beautiful I am and commanding me to come for him. Almost no words passed between us, but he spent hours making me feel loved and adored.

He wants me to wait for him, I can feel it in my bones. But I can't wait for him here. The smart move would be to take Pop's advice and live my life until Caleb comes back.

I get out of the truck, and I don't even make it to her porch when the door flings open, Smitten barreling toward me. Cassidy leans against the doorframe while I praise Smitten for being a good girl.

"So, when are you leaving?"

# ingrid

. . .

Two Weeks Later

"I absolutely loved *The Ruined Spitfire*, do you have any plans to make it into a movie or show?"

Amanda blushes. "No, I don't think I could do it. My husband was a bit of an inspiration for that one, and I wouldn't be able to handle the casting for it." Muting the video call, she talks to someone off the screen for a moment. When the little mute icon disappears, she asks, "When would you be able to start on *Maybe in Fifty?*"

I do my best to contain my excitement. "Right away. Just let me know if you need me to work from a studio space."

"Remote is fine until we start filming. I'll want you on set with me to make any necessary adjustments to the script. Romance Flix wants to start in January and have a summer release."

A man with a thick Scottish accent adds, "That timing is absolute *shite.*"

"Shh, I'm on a call," she whispers to him, then tells me, "He's right, but it's what we've got. We'll be filming in Los Angeles with one of their New York backdrops. So… are you in?"

"Yes," I try to say as calmly as I can. "Absolutely."

"Great! I'll contact the studio and have them send the contract over to your agent to review."

We say our goodbyes and hang up the video call. The moment the message hits on my end that the call has ended, I pump my fists in the air and scream, "Yes!" It scares Smitten, who paws at me. I rub behind her ear and laugh, "Sorry, Smits, but today is a good day."

Nerves overtake me, and I feel my breakfast rise from my stomach. I rush to the bathroom and throw up my delicious onion bagel with garlic and herb cream cheese. *Damn it!* Smitten nuzzles her snout against me as I get cleaned up.

As I'm brushing my teeth, I tell her, "It's okay, I'm just nervous. I got the job! It's a dream come true, pup." I finish freshening up and let her out back to run around.

Cay's backyard was open. With how rambunctious Smitten is, David had Mike fence it in for us. She needs space to run, and now she has a safe place to do it. While she's leaping around, trying to catch a butterfly, I go back inside to make a cup of coffee. As it's brewing, there's a knock at the door.

Cass lets herself in quietly, so I yell to her from the kitchen, "My call is over, I got *Maybe in Fifty!*"

She makes a beeline for me and nearly knocks me over with a hug. "I knew you would!" As awkward as everything is with Cay gone, she's still my biggest cheerleader.

"Thanks! I'll be checking my email every hour until I see the contract."

My phone pings on the counter, and I excitedly snatch it up, even though there's only a slim chance it's the contract. While it's probably junk email, I swipe anyway. As suspected, it's just an advertisement for body lotions and candles. My shoulders sag, and as I'm about to set it down, I notice an email two down from it with the subject line: Missed Appointment with Dr. Blake. I click on it, and the world stops. I was supposed to go in for my OBGYN appointment almost three weeks ago.

"Shit!"

"What?" Cassidy moves to the side of me to read over my shoulder. "Oh, that's no big deal, there are two OBs here who can fit you in for your pap."

"No," I cry. "I don't just go for my pap."

She pulls out her phone. "What do you need? Period issues? Need pelvic floor help? My friend is great, I'll see if I can get you in."

"*Cass.*"

"What?" She looks up, pausing for a moment. "Hold on… What birth control are you on?"

"The kind that requires an OB four times a year…"

We stare at each other for a moment. "It's okay! I'm sure it's fine. You probably weren't ovulating while Cay was still here." Cass shrugs and types on her phone. "I'll get you in to see my friend today, just to be safe."

"This can't be happening." I begin pacing, wringing my hands. "I've always been so careful, even used condoms, how did I let this happen?"

Cass grabs both my shoulders, forcing me to stop and look at her. "Perfect. You used condoms. It's going to be okay... You *did* use condoms, right?" My silence is admission enough for her. "Damn it, Ingrid! What about with the boss daddy?"

"Martin? Yes, we used a condom, but they aren't one-hundred percent."

"And Caleb?"

I wince. "No."

"It's okay, it'll be fine... Totally fine..." The high screech of her voice tells me it'll be everything but fine. "I got you in for this afternoon at three. Are you having any symptoms?"

"Like what?" I grasp at my stomach, not feeling any different.

"Insomnia, morning sickness, cravings..."

"No." I shake my head, but then my eyes widen. "I threw up my bagel this morning... but that's just nerves. I was just offered the job!"

Cass' shoulders sag as she gives me a knowing look. "Babe, I've been a nurse for years and have read a fuckton of accidental pregnancy romance books. You're probably knocked up. I'll run to the store to pick up a few tests, you'll pee on a stick, and we'll know for sure what's going on."

"Okay," I sigh, nodding my head in agreement.

She grabs her things and rushes to the store, leaving me to freak out alone. I let Smitten back inside, and she can sense my worry, not leaving my side. I do my best to manifest a negative test—speaking it into the universe over and over, hoping it'll take.

Fifteen minutes later, Cass rushes in with a plastic grocery bag full of tests. "Pick your poison. We've got the double-line tests, the ones with words, the cheap tests, and the expensive tests. I say you pee in a cup and we shove all twelve of them in there at once."

"Good plan."

"I'm kidding." Cass pulls out a plastic disposable cup from the cabinet. "We're going to eliminate the possibility of error here. Each box has two tests. So, you're going to pee now, we'll do one round. Then, in an hour or so, do another round. Okay?" I nod and take the cup from her, rushing off to the bathroom. Once I'm done, I return to the kitchen, urine in hand. "Bitch! Back in there! I'll come to you. We're not going to risk piss spilling in here."

I groan and return to the bathroom, Cass following me with a handful of unwrapped tests. Once I set the cup on the counter, she begins carefully placing them in. All of the packages say three to five minutes, so we decide to wait the full five.

It's the longest five minutes of my life.

The timer chimes, and I can't look. Cass pulls out the first one, capping it and setting it on a paper towel. "Ah-ha! Negative!" I breathe a sigh of relief. She pulls the second one out, and her eyes widen. "Oh, this one must be one of the cheap tests…"

"What does it say?"

"The line is faint, it could go either way."

I take the test from her and deadpan, "Those are two distinct lines, Cass."

She pulls the remaining tests, capping them and placing them on the paper towel. "Well… good news is one-sixth of these tests are negative."

"There are five positives!"

"Here me out… It could be anything! Your HCG levels could be off from your birth control."

Tears begin to fill my eyes, but I refuse to let them fall. "Cass… What if it's not Cay's?"

"It has to be." Cassidy wraps me in a tight hug. "The universe wouldn't be that cruel. You said the asshole used a condom, who did you sleep with before him?"

"No one for months," I whisper.

She pulls back. "See! But it doesn't matter who the father is. What do you want to do? I support you unless you want me to throw you down the stairs. Mostly because I don't know anyone who has a house with stairs."

"Damn, Cass. Brutal," I laugh and wipe a stray tear that

fell. "No, I don't need to be thrown down the stairs. But... I can't tell Caleb."

"Why not?" She frowns, and I cock an eyebrow at her. "Oh, right, he's off doing Navy shit."

"Yes, but no. It might not be his. I can't tell him until I know for sure."

"Statistically unlikely that it's not Caleb's."

"Cass," I warn.

"I mean, I get that you want to be sure, but can we just pretend it's his so I can be happy for you? Wait, should I be happy for you? I'm happy if you're happy. Why am I getting the feeling you're not? In which case... what do you want to do? Stairs aren't an option. Best I've got is a coat hanger, but it'll probably accidentally murder you, and I am *not* going to jail for that." She pauses for a moment in her word-vomit while I stifle a laugh. "Seriously, though, if you need me to go back to New York with you for *anything*. Just say the word."

"No." I shake my head. "If these tests are right, I'm financially stable enough to raise a child on my own."

Cass steps back with a look of shock as if I slapped her. "Um, excuse me. That little lima bean—or whatever weird vegetable or fruit they associate with it this early—is my niece or nephew. Doesn't matter if it's Caleb's or not, I'm Auntie Cass."

"I'm not dragging your brother into this," I insist. I'm overcome with a flood of emotions. I don't want Caleb to be eternally tied to me because of a child. I also don't want my child to grow up without a father. And I sure as hell don't want anyone resenting me for keeping a child I didn't plan for…

"Ingrid." Cass' stern tone pulls me from my spiral. "You don't need to decide anything right now. But, babe, we both know if you do those other six tests, statistically, they'll likely be positive. You'll talk to an OBGYN and see what they think, do a proper test, and when you get the results, you can make the big decisions."

A short moment of understanding passes between us, but it's rudely disrupted by my adorable but mischievous Dalmatian, stealing two of the pregnancy tests off the bathroom counter and spilling the plastic cup of pee all over her.

"Smitten," I call, reaching for her collar, but she's too quick for me. Cass is able to tackle her, tugging on her collar and bringing her back to the bathroom. "Damn it, Smit!" I snatch the tests out of her mouth.

"I'll give her a quick bath." Cass smells herself. "And me. Go take a long shower and overthink everything."

"I love you," I sigh.

"Love you, more," she replies, practically singing.

# caleb

...

D aniels has been blasting Disturbed and Godsmack for the past two weeks, to the point where I'm confident I know both bands' entire catalog. After helping a stranded submarine safely come to the surface, we've spent the last four days at sea, essentially twiddling our thumbs to ensure everything is going according to plan.

The one thing I hate about missions like these is no one knows about them unless someone leaks it. Being in the middle of fucking nowhere, no one can contact the media to tell them. Mostly, I want to discreetly get the message back to Ingrid, Pop, and Cass. Pop would put two and two together that I'm here and tell them.

In one *long* week, I'll be fully debriefed, and hopefully have a chance to talk to one of them. As soon as our reports are filed, I'll be able to start my two-year training program and get back to my girl.

One. More. Week.

"Can you turn that down?" I groan, prepping dinner in the galley kitchen. He can't hear me through the music, so I turn it off myself.

"It was just getting to the good part!"

With a roll of my eyes, I turn it back on at a lower volume. While Daniels is a fucking genius, and there are no words to describe how I am grateful for his help with the sub. I know he misses his girl back home, so the least I can do is let him listen to his favorite bands on repeat to keep his mind off it.

"Are you being a sad fuck again?" He exaggerates a pout.

Before I can answer, the entire ship shakes, and both of us brace ourselves. "What the fuck was that? Were we hit?"

We rush out of the galley and up to our stations as lights flash above us. Just in case, Daniels and I start suiting up for 'abandon ship.' No one has answers until the intercom confirms the dreaded words, bringing the nightmare to reality.

*Fuck!*

*There's no one out here, how did they not see something coming for us?*

No matter how many drills they put you through, various officers are shouting orders from fucking color-coded index cards, almost as if they have no clue what the hell we're supposed to do. The moment I'm in the lifeboat I hop out of it and shout, "Who here has kids at home? And I mean I better see fucking photos." Two seamen approach, these guys can't be a day over twenty. "Photos." They each retrieve pictures of them with their kids—one with a little boy, the other with two girls. "Get in."

Daniels yells, "What the fuck are you doing?"

I think back to Ingrid telling me she lost our child. The only thing worse than losing a child, is losing a spouse or parent. I won't let a child go without a father if I can help it.

A few other officers and I help fill all of the boats with fathers first, and thankfully, this isn't like some movie—there's space for everyone. I get into one of the last boats, and it lowers into the murky, dark ocean. I feel like we're sitting ducks out here, but I'm reassured by everyone that there's a ship on the way to us. I look back, finding ours still floating. I don't know how bad the damage is, but my instinct is to go back and fix it.

The motors carry us for miles until they nearly give out. From what I've gathered based purely on rumor, the sub we fixed glitched and set off a missile straight for us. I don't believe a word of it but continue to nod as the story is told and retold to me.

A ship comes into view six hours later, and my hope is temporarily restored. I won't be able to rest until I'm home with my family around me.

Once we board, I'm interviewed by four different officers, each hoping for a different answer. I wish I had a better one to give. A story of being in a kitchen galley, then being hit by an alleged rogue missile, isn't the story people want to hear. So, I patiently await the official statement they expect me to share.

Not wanting us to mingle our stories, I'm essentially kept in solitary confinement until they deem me fit for somewhere else. They claim it's not a holding cell, but there's no other description for it. I'm allowed nothing—except pencil and paper. Choosing my words wisely, I write to my girl.

*Ingrid,*

*I never expected these past few weeks to happen like they did. I don't know when I'll be able to see you again, but if this reaches you, please know that I'll do everything I can to get back to you.*

*Always yours,*
*Caleb*

I read and reread the note, ensuring there's no way it could be construed as a secret message. If there's any way they can get it to her, I might be able to sleep tonight.

As I hand it to an officer, they ask, "Who is Ingrid?"

"My wife," I answer, matter-of-factly, even if the lie eats at me. I'm not under oath, so it shouldn't come back to haunt me. I am just hoping that he takes pity on me.

"Your current address?"

I nod, and he leaves, but based on his tone my letter will never reach her.

# ingrid

. . .

"You're a little too early for a traditional ultrasound to confirm, but with your elevated HCG levels, it's highly likely that you're pregnant."

Cass squeezes my hand and asks the doctor, "But it could mean that she's not, right?"

"We can try a transvaginal ultrasound to see if anything comes up?" she offers.

"What's that?" I ask, but I'm pretty sure she'll be shoving something up my snatch.

"We'll use an ultrasound wand and insert it inside you. It's a bit uncomfortable, but it will give us a better image if you're only seven or eight weeks pregnant. It will also catch things like a blighted ovum, or other conditions that will give a positive pregnancy test without an active pregnancy."

"Oh. Yes, let's do that." I nod nervously. "I need to know for sure."

The doctor preps the wand, and as I place my feet in the stirrups, she has me breathe while pressing it inside me. It's uncomfortable, but not any worse than a pap exam.

The screen looks like static until a large black spot appears. "That's your uterus." She moves the wand a little and points at the screen where a little static outline appears. "And that? Let's see…" Squinting at her computer, she measures the small outline. "Just over a third of an inch. Seven and a half weeks feels accurate." She clicks a few more times and finally says the words I've been expecting, "You're definitely pregnant. There's a faint heartbeat, but that will be stronger in the next few weeks."

I hold Cass' hand tighter and whisper, "What am I going to do?"

Cass asks louder, "What are her options?"

My doctor gives Cass a look of warning, then softens her features as she tells me, "The only assistance I can provide is prenatal care and information about adoption options. Should you need *other* healthcare needs regarding the pregnancy, it might be best to go home and speak with your OBGYN there."

I don't miss the implication. If I wanted to terminate the pregnancy, I couldn't do it here. While that might be an option other women consider in my situation, I'm not. Cass is right, it's probably Caleb's, but I have to be honest with him in case it isn't.

Amanda said I can work remotely until filming. I do quick math in my head, and I'll be almost eight months pregnant on set. That isn't exactly something I can hide. Fuck, my water could break in the middle of a scene.

"You're pale," Cass notes, looking me over. "Need me to grab a water, a snack... What do you need?"

I try not to laugh, thinking about the last night with Caleb. Maybe attentiveness is hereditary. "I'm okay, I just need a minute." I then tell the doctor, "I'll need a full list of what I should be doing—vitamins, supplements, etcetera. As well as a list of things to avoid. I had a miscarriage when I was eighteen, I don't want to experience that again."

Cass gasps, whisper-shouting, "What?" while my doctor exhales a sigh of relief, likely because I'm avoiding the big conversations she has to have with some patients.

"You'll want to set up regular check-ups with an OBGYN to monitor everything. Prenatal vitamins are important, but personally, I also like to make sure my patients are eating a balanced diet that will keep their body and immune system in the best condition possible. If you workout regularly, you can usually keep the same routine for the next several months, but you won't want to start anything new..." As she continues to list everything, I space out, overwhelmed by the information. She places her hand on mine, bringing me back to the present, and I'm unsure of how long I was dissociating. "It's a lot. I'll send you home with information, but if you're going to be here for the next few weeks, I'd like to set up a follow-up appointment with you. If not with me, with the other OB on staff."

"Thanks, Steph," Cass tells her. Checking her phone, she sucks in a breath. "Oh, shit, I have to get to the bar and cover for Lo for an hour. Want to come by for a drink?" When I don't answer, she laughs, "Oh, right, water it is!" Her eyes wide, she corrects, "Shit! No! Not water. That would bring a lot of weird questions at the bar. Um... ginger ale, I'll pour you a ginger ale."

I laugh at her gaff and agree to join her later; I need to get home and check on Smitten. Cass insists I bring her with me and stick to the patio. The weather has been working in our favor this week, so it should be a nice night to sit out back at the bar and watch the sunset.

So, that's exactly what I do.

After several hours on the patio with Smitten, the sun is nearly behind the mountains, and the crisp lake air chills me. I tie Smitten to a pole for a minute to walk inside and tell Cass I'm headed home.

I only make it a few steps when I notice the bar is eerily quiet, everyone's attention on the television. Moving closer, I see the headline: Mayday for Naval Ship in the Pacific.

*Caleb.*

"Cass, what's going on?"

She turns, fear etched in her eyes. "I don't know. They evacuated a ship. No casualties."

I breathe a brief sigh of relief. "And Cay?"

Cassidy rounds the bar and hugs me, whispering low enough that only I can hear. "Pop said he couldn't confirm what the ship was doing but that Cay was on it."

"Fuck," I cry. "Is he okay?"

"We don't know. Pop is waiting by the phone for answers. He can't tell me anything, but it sounds like Caleb's all right." She releases me and adds, "Take Smitten home, and I'll let you know if I hear anything. You need to rest. Do you want me to have Pop come by?"

"No, I'll be okay. Please call me if you hear anything?"

"I promise."

# caleb

. . .

"The ship didn't sink," I mutter to the tenth person who has interviewed me today. I didn't even bother to get his name, it doesn't matter.

"Start at the beginning."

I walk through it again, but at the end, as I expect them to be unsatisfied and leave, they ask, "Can you help us fix it?"

"What?" My eyes widen; he's the first one to ask me about the ship's condition and not imply it's at the bottom of the ocean.

"Can you help us fix it?" he repeats. "In every other interview we've done, they claim it sank. It's still standing, but the lower levels are flooded. You're one of four people we know of who have the skills to do it. I can't tell you how it happened, but we want to salvage an asset that costs a quarter of a billion dollars."

"If I don't know how it happened, how can I fix it?"

"The engineers are estimating six months to get it back home. If you join their team, we'll renegotiate your contract to end after a year. Six months at sea, six months shore duty."

*I'll get back to Ingrid faster…*

"Done," I reply confidently without a second thought.

He frowns, likely expecting a fight. "We'll draw up a new contract. In the meantime, intelligence will brief you with official statements. With the sensitivity of the project, you won't be able to return home until it's over. We can allow your family to visit you for the thirty-six hours we're on base before shipping out. But it'll be supervised and you'll have someone assigned to you until you leave."

"Understood."

With a curt nod, he stands, and I do the same, saluting him. "Thank you for your service." He turns on his heel to leave.

Before he opens the door, I rush out, "Please ensure my father, David Rogers, my sister, Cassidy Rogers, and my… *wife*, Ingrid Lawrence, are invited to base."

He nods again and steps out of the room. Unlike the note I wanted to reach her, I'm feeling more confident that my family will actually be invited to base before I leave.

―――――――

Two days later, and after another restless night's sleep, I wake to a banging on the door before it swings open and someone announces, "Ten minutes," before shutting it. We must be nearly at port, and I'm curious to see if anyone will be here for me. I rush to make my bed and dress, anxiously waiting on the door to unlock a second time.

After several minutes, it opens, and three highly decorated officers step in. "Commander Rogers."

"Yes, Sir." I salute then move to 'at ease' when prompted. I'm used to seamen saluting me, not the other way around, so I'm a bit rusty.

"Thirty-six hours begins now." He turns on his heel, and the other two officers wait for me to follow.

We leave the ship and enter one of the buildings next to the landing dock. No one is here. It's quiet, too quiet. We walk down several sterile hallways until we reach an unmarked door. He stands to the side of it expectantly, and I open it.

I don't make it a foot inside before my sister's arms are wrapped around my neck. I immediately find Ingrid standing a few feet away next to Pop, looking less than pleased with me.

"Thank fuck you're okay!" Cass cries.

"I'm okay," I assure her, holding her tighter, my eyes not leaving my Ingrid. I pull Cass' arms down from around my neck and stalk over to my girl, not giving a fuck who might be watching. I take her face in my hands and roughly kiss her. It takes her by surprise, but her gasp quickly becomes a sigh against my lips, and she pulls me closer.

Pop clears his throat. "Son, now might be a good time to tell your *wife* why we are here?"

I groan as I pull away from Ingrid, already missing the taste of her. I take a quick inventory of my surroundings: two cameras and a one-way mirror. I carefully tell her, "I'm leaving for a few months, so they allowed me to see my *family* before I go." I press a kiss to her cheek and whisper softly, "I'm sorry, it was the only way I could see you. Please play along, they're watching."

"How long are you going for?" Pop grumbles.

"They are splitting my contract. Six at sea, six on shore." Ingrid stiffens against me, but I keep her close. "I won't have contact with anyone while I'm at sea, so I asked to see you all before I go."

"That's what the officer said before you came in," Ingrid says quietly. "We should've left it the way we did back home. This? This is harder."

"Why don't we give you two some privacy?" Cass offers, then laughs, "Well, sort of." She waves and talks at the mirror. "Hi there! Can he have some alone time with his wife? No? Okay, well, I'm going to step out in case things are about to get spicy in here. Enjoy the show, boys!" She pats me on the back. "They said we're allowed to have a supervised lunch with you. Are you sure you're not some kind of inmate? This is giving me prison vibes."

Pop rolls his eyes. "All right, that's enough." He guides her out of the room. "We'll see you in a bit."

The door shuts, and Ingrid's cool expression is replaced with worry. "I have to tell you something, and I'm pretty sure you're not going to want to see me again after I tell you."

My stomach drops, and my chest tightens. Ingrid takes a step back. This is it, she's walking away.

She casts her eyes down. "I'm pregnant." My gaze falls to her belly, my heart shifting from dread to swelling with so much love for this woman and our unborn child.

"Ingrid," I breathe.

A rogue tear leaves her eye. I reach for her, but she takes another step back. "I need to do a paternity test while you're here."

"It… it's not mine?" I take a seat in one of the cold metal chairs.

Ingrid steps closer and falls to her knees in front of me. "What I'm about to tell you is why you'll never want to see me again."

"Then, I don't want to hear it," I snap. She shuts her eyes tight with a wince, as if I slapped her. "Fuck, I'm sorry." Taking her hands in mine, I kiss her palms and rest one on my chest above my heart. "Even if it hurts, tell me."

She blows out a long breath. "It's about why I came home in the first place." She recounts a story about how her boss came onto her and how she felt she had no choice but to sleep with him. All I hear is a man who abused his power and took advantage of the woman I love. As she continues telling me what happened, I do my best to contain the rage building inside me.

I don't blame Ingrid for what he did to her. I'm sure she wasn't the first woman he slept with who quit shortly after, either out of embarrassment or after being forced out of her job. The only thing that matters now is that he'll never touch her again for as long as I live. If this child is his, I'll do everything in my power to make sure he doesn't come within a hundred miles of Ingrid and the baby.

"We used a condom, but there's a small chance… I'm so sorry, Cay."

For all our lives, I've almost never seen Ingrid cry. As kids, she broke her leg; not a sob. As teens, she didn't even shed a tear at the saddest of movies or books. Now, as adults, she sits before me as one of the strongest women I know, on her knees and eyes swollen with hurt she's trying to hold back.

"I don't care if it's his."

"Will you take the test?" she asks softly. "To be sure?"

I swipe her tears from her cheeks with my thumbs and brush a gentle kiss to her lips. "I'll do it for you. I know we'll have a lot to talk about when I'm back, but you're mine, Ingrid, and that means this baby is mine, too."

Covering my hands with hers, she shakes her head. "I don't want you to do this because you feel you have to. I'll be okay."

"In case you have forgotten"—I glance at the mirror and back to Ingrid, then smile—"you're my wife. My bucket list, *my life*, begins and ends with you."

Ingrid is about to reply when there's a knock at the door. "Rogers. You and your wife can have lunch with the rest of your family, and visit the medical clinic. Then, we need to begin briefings."

My shoulders sag in defeat that our time is almost up. This will be the longest six months of my life. Despite it all, one thing's for certain, the moment it's over, I'm spending the rest of my days with Ingrid as my wife.

# ingrid

# . . .

"Back to your swoony declarations for my best friend, I see," Cass jests, elbowing Caleb in the side. "I saw the huge book delivery, not sure where she's going to put all of those paperbacks. I should store them at my place. You know, be a good sister and all."

"It was really too much," I confess.

Caleb's hand slides into mine under the table. "I had Daniels download the books onto my device, and I felt like a book pirate. He suggested I get the physical copies to ease my conscience."

"Uh, there was alien smut in there," Cass deadpans, making Pop choke on his own air. "Easy, Pop, that's just the tip of the iceberg. You should've seen some of the Daddy Dom titles."

"Cass!" I shriek. "I'm so sorry, Mr. Rogers. I assure you there were no Daddies in my book delivery."

"You know better than to call me that," he groans. When Cass snorts a laugh, he clarifies, "Mr. Rogers was my father. But if you don't mind, can we change the subject?"

Cay explains, "I left my device on the ship, before it"—the officer babysitting us glares at him in warning—"died." He clears his throat and doubles down, "Before the *device died*. I'm going to need a new NERD, and order another ereader for Ingrid, too."

"I'll make sure your wifey has a new one," Cass insists, sipping her iced tea.

"Anyway," I draw out. "Caleb and I should get going. We need to get the lab tests done here before he has to leave."

"We don't have to, I told you I don't care," he huffs.

"I know, but I do." I pull my hand back and stand. "I'll see you guys after?"

It's going to be rough with Caleb gone. His dad was right, he loves big, and when he sets his mind on something, he's determined. But, I refuse to let him feel obligated to be with me, let alone get married, because of a child.

Caleb gets up and follows me out of the glorified cafeteria. I look around, finding happy families with their escorts. I'm not sure I like the idea of having our child having these sorts of chaperoned visits.

The walk to the medical building is quiet. Caleb insists on holding my hand, maybe to keep up appearances since he has claimed I'm his wife. While I understand that he lied to ensure he was able to see me, it doesn't make it easy on me. We didn't end things well, so much left unsaid. It's easy to be swept up in him, even easier to live in the fantasy where we're essentially playing house. My heart aches for him, but my head refuses to let me fall until we have a chance to take our time.

*I'm pregnant. And he's leaving. What time do we have?*

"Name?" the woman barks at the entrance of the medical center.

"Ingrid Lawrence and Caleb Rogers."

She checks her tablet. "Thank you, go ahead inside."

Caleb opens the door for me, guiding me in by the small of my back. The simple touch lights me up, as it always has— or maybe that's just the pregnancy hormones talking. We check in at the desk and take a seat. Caleb takes my hand, interlaces our fingers, and brings my knuckles to his lips. I can't help letting out a long breath.

"Fuck, I'm going to miss you," he whispers.

Rubbing my other hand over his smooth cheek, I tease, "I miss the beard," hoping to lighten the mood.

"I'll grow it out again, as soon as we're back home." He smiles widely, and *damn*, I've missed that smile.

"About that… I'm staying at your place—"

"*Our* place," he corrects with a side glance at our shadow.

"Right. Well, I'm staying there, but I was offered head writer for the *Maybe in Fifty* mini-series for Romance Flix. They want me in Los Angeles in January."

Caleb pulls me in close and kisses my temple. "Fuck, that's amazing! I'm so fucking proud of you."

"Did you just skip over that last part? I'm moving in January."

He thinks for a moment before responding, "I'll be starting my shore duty in January. I'll see about being stationed in San Diego, so I'll only be two hours from you. Unless…"

"Unless, what?"

"Stay on base with me? I can probably look into what family housing is there, but we would have to"—he kisses my cheek and whispers—"get married for real." My body stiffens. While I see myself marrying him one day, I'm not ready.

"Lawrence. Rogers," a woman calls from the side door next to the reception desk. Caleb and I stand and walk in, his hand never leaving mine. "We'll start by getting height and weight." She checks both, and we continue down the hall into a small examination room. "Your doctor will be in shortly."

The man who has been following us since I got here tries to enter the room with us. "I'm sorry, I know you're trying to do your job. But could Caleb and I please have a moment alone when the doctor comes in?"

"I'm afraid I can't allow that."

"My wife deserves her privacy," Caleb growls.

"If you need time alone with the doctor, Rogers will need to exit with me."

I squeeze Caleb's hand and tell the man, "It's just a little embarrassing discussing prenatal testing with a stranger. I suppose you're used to your medical records being out in the open?"

The doctor enters. "Good afternoon. We're here for paternity testing today?" She glances between Caleb and our stalker-bodyguard. "Oh, I'll need to grab more swabs."

"No," I laugh. "Just Caleb."

Not pressing any further, she instead goes on to tell us that she'll be testing for blood type and a variety of conditions like anemia. She then collects blood samples and cheek swabs from Caleb and me. When we're done, she jokes, "Are you sure you don't want to test this one?" She gestures with her thumb, and Caleb and I laugh.

"No, thank you though."

"Great. You're free to go, we'll send the results in a few days."

As we leave, Caleb stops me in the waiting room, takes me in his arms, and kisses my temple—just another thing I've missed—then reminds me, "It doesn't matter."

I don't know why I keep fighting this. The most amazing man I've ever known is telling me he would spend the rest of his life raising a child who might not be his. I know in my heart it is, but seeing it in black and white will help my nerves about all of it.

The damn shadow clears his throat. "We need to get back if you want to say goodbye to your sister and father."

Caleb keeps me close and tells me softly, "When I'm back in December, we'll figure everything out, I promise."

We return the same way we came to find Pop and Cass. Once we reach them, Cay hugs them both and assures them he'll be safe. He then wraps an arm around me and leans me back like something out of a damn movie, pausing before kissing me. I let out a full laugh at his ridiculousness until his lips crash into mine in a searing kiss; I moan on contact.

"Your dad is right there," I mutter against him.

He pulls me upright and replies, "I don't fucking care." Pressing his forehead to mine, he sighs, "You're my everything, Ingrid." He splays his hand on my belly. "Both of you are. I love you."

And, for the first time, I admit, "I love you, too."

# caleb

. . .

Three Months Later

Ingrid,

We got some good news today! I know you'll be reading these in one large batch when I get home, but writing to you daily makes it feel like you're here with me. I can't share the news, but Pitz and I made some great headway with the project and there's a light at the end of the tunnel—so to speak.

Twenty-one weeks pregnant today. My calendar says our baby is measuring around ten inches, the size of a carrot. By now, you've probably gone in for an ultrasound and got to see our sweet baby boy or girl. Fuck, I miss you both so much. The next few months are going to be torture.

I hope Smitten isn't giving you too much

trouble and Travis has helped if you need it. I hope you're safe and I'm counting down the days until I'm home.

Always yours,
Caleb

# caleb

. . .

One Month Later

Ingrid,

Today was hard. No. It fucking sucked. We spent twelve hours working on creating a patch that wouldn't take. I'm fucking exhausted. I blacked out twice, and while I don't remember what happened, my first thought when I woke up was that I hope you and our baby are safe.

Tomorrow will be better.

Twenty-five weeks, sweetheart. By now, you might know if we're having a boy or a girl. Did you find out? We should've talked about it before I left, but I'm dying to know. I can't wait to start picking out furniture and to paint the nursery. Do you want a nursery? Some of the guys here say that co-sleeping is a thing. I'm not in love with the idea of sharing our bed with a little one. I'd be

afraid I'd accidentally roll over onto it in my sleep.
But, if it's what you want to do, I'm in.

Always yours,
Caleb

# caleb

. . .

Six Weeks Later

Ingrid,

We're on our way back home! We've been promised that our families will be welcoming us in San Diego. I'll admit, I'm nervous you won't show.

I just finished a book about a billionaire and an accidental pregnancy that Pitz said you've probably read. Sorry, sweetheart, you didn't get the jackpot with me. The Navy doesn't hand out billions. You'll need to find a sugar daddy.

That was a joke. For the love, don't find a sugar daddy. I don't share, Ingrid.

The calendar says our baby is a coconut. Not sure that makes sense, that's smaller than sixteen inches. I think my calendar is broken.

I love you so fucking much, it hurts. In ten short days, we start the rest of our lives.

Irene Bahrd

*Always yours,*
*Caleb*

# ingrid

. . .

The last ten days have been torture, but each hour that passes is one closer to seeing Caleb. When Pop got the call, he assured me I was invited, even if no one called me. There's a chance they figured out I'm not actually Caleb's wife. I just hope it didn't get him into any trouble.

Before my feet even hit the floor, the front door opens, and Cass sings, "Ingrid! Today's the day!" I'm used to her waltzing in here whenever she pleases, it's the one thing I've come to expect these past months.

Smitten leaps off the bed and runs to the front door to greet her well before I ever could. I'm bloated, and fat, and uncomfortable, and severely under-caffeinated. I finally make my way to the kitchen, where Cassidy has two coffees in a carrier sitting on the counter.

"Fuck, you're a goddess," I moan, taking one of them. She snatches it back from me. "Hey!"

"Let me just check... Nope, that's mine." Handing me the other, she asks, "What are you going to wear?"

"A tent."

"Ingrid," she warns. "You're beautiful, will you stop that?"

I escalate. "A four-person tent should do it."

Cass groans. "That's it, we're going shopping on the way to the airport."

"Good idea. Might find a deal on a circus tent that I can grow into."

She marches into the bedroom and into the closet, pulling out a form-fitting, black dress I bought the other day. "Here. This one."

"Absolutely not."

Tossing it onto the bed, she frowns. "Why not?"

"My tits practically spill out of it."

Cass glances down to my giant breasts that refuse to be contained. "I fail to see the problem."

I roll my eyes and strip out of my drawstring pajama bottoms and one of Caleb's tees. It no longer smells like him, neither do his pillows, but it helps me feel close to him. I pull on the dress, look in the mirror, and sigh. My tits do look good, but my body isn't the same as when Caleb last saw me.

"You look amazing," she coos, then rests her chin on my shoulder looking in the mirror with me. "Did you write to him today?"

"No, I just got up. I'm going to see him later, I don't think I need to write to him."

She pulls out my leather-bound notebook and a pen from the bedside table. "Last letter."

I take them and walk back into the kitchen to sit at the island.

*Dear Caleb,*

*Hope this finds you well? What am I supposed to say to the man I'm going to see later? This whole thing feels ridiculous. It's been almost six months to the day since I saw you and these letters have served as more of a diary entry for me. I think your dad was onto something. If Cass doesn't tell you about them, I'll probably just hide this notebook in a drawer somewhere. Never to be seen again.*

*I'm nervous to see you after everything. Cass says I'm beautiful, but I feel like a whale. I just hope you're attracted to large sea mammals. Black is flattering, but there's no hiding the fact that I'm not the same woman I was months ago.*

*It doesn't change the fact that not a day has gone by that I haven't missed you. Our time together was short, but it felt like a lifetime. We have a million things to talk about, but today, can we just enjoy each other? Just for a day?*

*I've made a bucket list that I'll share with you one day.*

*If you still want me.*

*xoxo,*
*Ingrid*

I return to the bedroom and tuck the notebook under the bed where I hope Caleb won't look. I'm not even sure if he's coming back home before his shore duty, but better to be safe than embarrassed. Pop was right, writing to him every day has helped me work through it all.

After primping in the bathroom for entirely too long, I grab my suitcase and join Cass in the kitchen, and she leashes up Smitten to drop him off at Travis' on our way out of town. With a deep breath, I walk to the car and silently pray to myself that the man who fell in love with me six months ago still does.

# caleb

. . .

**W**e step off the ship, and my nerves are fucking shot. It's been nearly six months since I've seen her, held her in my arms, told her I love her…

*What if she doesn't show?*

*What if the baby is that asshole's and she's with him now?*

*What if she doesn't love me anymore?*

*What if she never did?*

"Rogers." Pitz's voice pulls my attention from my freak out.

"Yeah?"

"She'll be here," she assures me, though I know she's equally anxious. Her boyfriend is stationed here, and she hasn't seen him since we left. Time at sea changes you.

We make it through debrief meeting after debrief meeting and have been assured we have thirty days off before our shore duty. A month is plenty to help get everything ready for the baby, and hopefully move Ingrid out to San Diego or Los Angeles.

But it's also not enough with her.

After we finish with intelligence, Pitz and I make our way to the large gymnasium where they are holding our welcome party with the rest of the crew. As we approach, Pitz's boyfriend, Jones, jogs up to us and hugs her tightly, swinging her around twice before setting her down. He kisses her briefly, then whispers something in her ear. I can't help the small chuckle that escapes me watching them, but my eyes widen when he drops to one knee in front of us and proposes right on the spot.

I couldn't be more excited for her. These past months, she's become one of my closest friends and confidants. If he's half the man she's made him out to be, he'll make her happy. Though, my heart stills at the thought that Ingrid isn't ready for marriage, even though I am.

We walk inside, and I take a few photos with Pitz, including one where I'm fake-gasping and pointing at the ring. I wrap her in a tight hug until I hear the one voice that brings me peace like nothing else.

"Gone six months and already engaged?"

I've never turned so fast in my life. Though her tone is teasing, I can't imagine being with anyone other than Ingrid. In an instant, I take her in my arms, refusing to let go. *Fuck, she smells like home.* I can't take it a moment longer, and our mouths collide in a kiss that makes my heart stop.

"Whoa, careful. Your fiancée might get jealous." She smiles against my lips. "I guess you missed me?"

I slide a hand into her hair and tug to pull her back an inch. "I more than missed you… and *you*." I fall to one knee and press a kiss to her full belly.

Ingrid rakes her fingers through my hair and whispers, "She's yours, Cay."

"She?" I look up at her, and I have to hold back tears. Not because she's mine, but because we're going to have a perfect baby girl. Though, I suspect I would react the same if she said we were having a boy. Ingrid nods her head, biting her lip. "We're having a girl?"

I take a moment to drink in Ingrid—the mother of my child, the love of my life, the one woman I want to spend forever with. How she's even more beautiful than I remember is unfathomable. I swear she's glowing.

"Yeah, we're having a girl," she whispers.

"Is this her?" Pitz asks behind me.

I stand, wrapping one arm around Ingrid's shoulder and resting a hand on her belly. "Yes, this is Ingrid. Ingrid, this is Sam Pitz."

"Pleasure to—"

Pitz nearly knocks Ingrid over with a hug. "I'm so excited to finally meet you!" She pulls back. "This is my *fiancé*, Dan. He just proposed." Squealing she adds, "Fuck, I love calling him that. Can we go out to celebrate? Where are your dad and sister?"

Ingrid points to the other side of the gym, and they wave. I reply, "I should probably go see them. Rain check on the celebration?"

"I'm going to hold you to it."

Ingrid and I head in the direction of Cass and Pop, and she asks under her breath, "Is it okay that I'm here? I didn't get the call."

I stop us in our tracks and turn her to face me. "You, Ingrid Lawrence, are my family. Just as much as they are, if not more. I don't know why they didn't call, but if I had any say in it, I would've called you first."

"Cay..."

"Ingrid..." I mock, and she laughs. "I thought I was clear before I left."

"It's not that simple." She looks down at our perfect child growing inside her, and I tilt her chin to look at me. "We have to start over."

"I know." I bring her close and kiss her temple; she hums in response. "It doesn't change that I love both of you."

Ingrid nods, and we continue toward Pop and Cass. As soon as the sea of people parts enough, Cass comes rushing to me, wrapping her arms around my neck. "Cay, I swear to fuck if you screw things up with Ingrid..." I laugh, and she pinches my shoulder. "I'm serious. Don't mess this up."

Cass pulls back, and Pop brings me in for a tight hug. "I heard what you did. Good job, son."

His clearance is high enough to know the work I did out there. He'd never tell Cass or Ingrid, and the fact that he's held onto this for months makes my stomach knot. To know your son was in the middle of nowhere fixing a ship that everyone thought had sank—if things had gone wrong, he'd know in the worst possible way. I wouldn't wish that knowledge on anyone.

I knew Pop wrote to my mother every day he was gone, but now that I have Ingrid and we're expecting, it brings a whole other meaning. If I didn't make it, Pitz would ensure Ingrid had my journal with her letters—showing Ingrid how much I loved her. The men who go back for years with their wives and children at home have always had my respect, but never as much as I have in this moment.

The few minutes greeting Pop and Cass were too many. My entire body aches to be near Ingrid, and I take her in my arms again. She clutches her belly and chuckles, "Cay, you're home. You have a whole month with us."

"It's not enough," I sigh.

"What do you say we grab a bite to eat and check in at the hotel?" Pop asks, clamping his hand on my shoulder.

"Yeah, okay," I mutter, not letting Ingrid go.

"Cay," she whispers, "it's okay, we're here."

I take a deep breath and kiss her once before following Pop and Cass out of the gymnasium. A part of me has to be touching her, whether it be holding her hand, or guiding her down a narrow path. I can't not touch her. Part of me is afraid I'll wake up, and she'll disappear.

The plane overhead is low enough that the building rumbles. I grab Ingrid and press her against the wall, shielding her from whatever might fall around us.

"Son, it's ok," Pop assures me, holding both my shoulders.

I pull my head up to find Ingrid's wide eyes searching mine. My breath is erratic, heart beating out of my fucking chest, my body feeling like it's jumping out of its skin. It's what it felt like before I blacked out on the ship...

*What the fuck is happening?*

"What do you see?" Pop asks.

My eyes not leaving hers, it takes a moment before I reply, "Ingrid."

"Good. What do you smell?"

I swallow hard and breathe in. "Home."

He stifles a chuckle. "It's the daffodils she planted right outside your porch, son. What do you hear?"

"You talking to me."

"You're doing great. What do you feel?"

Ingrid places my hand on her stomach, and our daughter kicks against it. A whimpered sob tears through me, my heart still thumping in my ears. "Our daughter."

"Great job, Cay. Take ten deep breaths with me." I do as he asks, and by the eighth breath, I no longer hear the creaking of the ship around us. "Five more." I breathe in and out five more times, Ingrid keeping me present. "We'll stay here all night if we need to. We'll leave when you're ready."

"I'm ready." *I'm not.*

Ingrid's irises are blown, but not with fear, with worry. I did this to her. "Cay," she says lovingly but hesitantly takes my cheek in her hand, "I'm here. What do you need?"

I force my mind from darkness and bring myself back to her, remembering the last night we spent together. I don't need to touch her, be inside her, or taste her.

I just need… "You."

# ingrid

. . .

T hat's a big fucking ask.

*You?*

*What does he mean?*

I thought I was clear about the whole not marrying because of a child part, but apparently, I wasn't. Surely, he can't mean he wants to fuck me; I'm the size of an elephant. How could he want that? We haven't seen each other in six months, and he just freaked out about a plane overhead.

I've heard about men coming back from wars and missions, with a diagnosis list a mile long. Even Pop warned me Cay might be different. I should've seen the signs when we were in the gymnasium—the bags under his eyes, his reaction to finding out we're having a girl... He hasn't slept in who the fuck knows how long.

"Cay, you're safe," Pop insists, keeping his hands firmly on Caleb's shoulders.

With one hand bracing himself against the wall and his other on my belly, Caleb's eyes pierce me with a swirl of love and fear. "Not until they're safe."

"Rogers. You're safe. Ingrid's safe. Your child is safe," Pop commands, making Caleb's posture rigid.

I hate that this is his military response and instinctively wrap my arms around his middle. I keep my cheek pressed against his chest until his heart rate slows, then softly reassure him, "You're safe. I'm here. Our baby is safe… You're safe, Caleb."

He kisses the top of my head and whispers, "I'm sorry."

"What do you feel?" I repeat Pop's words and place his hand back onto my belly.

"Our daughter," he sighs against me.

"We're safe. You made sure we're safe."

"I love you… so much."

The desperation in his voice pierces my heart with a thousand daggers. I don't know what he's going through, all of this is foreign to me. This isn't the Caleb I've known or the one I fell for. I need him back. "What do you need, Cay?"

"You. I need home."

What I thought would be a sweet, picturesque moment seeing each other today, has ended up with the strongest man I've known pleading for my safety, which already exists. He'll need help, more than I can give, but the best I've got right now is to get him far away from anything that might set off an episode like he just experienced.

"Cass," I whimper, "can you make sure our room is ready?"

Pop replies before she does, "I already checked in on the app. We can use our phones to unlock the door."

"Since when are you tech-savvy?" Cass laughs.

I can't help the small laugh that escapes me, even though Caleb's face is still buried in my neck. "Did you hear that? Your dad figured out an app all by himself. No reading glasses required."

"Hey!" Pop teases.

"Cay, whenever you're ready, we can leave," I say softly.

"One more minute."

"Of course," I whisper, pressing a soft kiss to his cheek as our daughter kicks against his hand. His eyes soften, breathing steadies, appearing more like my Caleb by the second.

Several pass and Cay finally rights his posture. "I'm sorry."

I cup his neck and bring his lips to mine. Between kisses, I manage, "No apologies. We'll make sure you have someone to talk to about this, but for now, you're safe with me, Pop, and Cass."

I didn't anticipate Cay's mental health to be added to my laundry list of things that need attention before our daughter was born. But in less than one day, it has shot to the top of it.

"Let's get you home, son," Pop says carefully, but Caleb doesn't move.

"Cay, I'm safe. Pop is here. Both of you will make sure me and the baby are safe, okay? Do you want to talk to someone now or in the morning?" He doesn't reply; he's so rigid I'm afraid to move him. "Hey, Pop, why don't we have Cass find us a doctor on-site while we wait?"

"Happy to," Cass pipes up. "I'll be back in a few."

Cassidy leaves, while Pop keeps his grip firmly placed on Cay's shoulders. "It's okay, Pop." He brushes them away slowly and I wrap my arms around Caleb. Pop then places a hand on the center of Caleb's back as I remind Cay, "I'm here. Our baby is safe."

"I'm sorry. So sorry," he mutters over and over, my heart breaking that he feels he could be at fault for any of this.

"Please don't apologize. You protected me. You protected our baby. You protected our family. You're safe." The command in my voice surprises even me. Even Pop has to hide his smirk. "Let's get you home."

# caleb

. . .

I try my hardest to stay grounded, but fear keeps seeping in. The emotional toll is fucking exhausting. "All I want is a night with my wife."

Ingrid looks to Pop, pupils dilated and little wrinkles forming between her eyes. Ingrid isn't my wife, but for the past six months it's what I had to hang onto.

"I mean—"

"Cay, we're staying together tonight. If that's what you want," Ingrid offers. It's not placating; she wants to stay with me. My heart rate slows from knowing this was her plan all along.

It takes me a beat to remember her words, *"She's yours, Cay."*

*Our daughter.*

"Rogers," Pop warns.

I tear my eyes away from her for the first time in what feels like hours. "Is she safe?"

"Yes," Pop insists. "Ingrid and your daughter are safe." *They keep telling me this, why don't I believe it?* He then tells Ingrid, "Why don't you and Cass check in at the hotel? Caleb and I will be there soon."

"I'm not leaving—"

"Ingrid," he snaps. "Hotel."

"No," she bites back, her eyes murderous. "Not until I know Caleb is okay."

"I'm okay," I whisper. "But... Pop is right." I hold Ingrid close, and as much as it hurts to admit, I sigh, "I need to talk to someone before I stay the night with you. If I ever hurt you or our baby—"

"You wouldn't," she declares defiantly.

"I can't risk it."

Pop places his hand on her shoulder, and she shoots him a warning glare. His voice gentler, he tells her, "Ingrid, trust me. Go to the hotel. We'll call you as soon as he can talk to someone."

The creaking overhead continues and sends me right back to the galley kitchen when we were hit. Suddenly, another flashback to the patch failing fills my mind. The rushing water, the boat breaking beneath me. My ears are ringing, and I try my hardest to stay present. Pop keeps a hand pressed firmly on my back as I try to control my breathing.

Tears fall from the woman who never cries. "They never called me." No matter how hard she tries to hold them back, Ingrid's tears track down her cheeks. It makes my own eyes swell and tears threaten to fall. "Please."

"Rogers. Lawrence." Pop's voice is now stern; both Ingrid's and my postures stiffen. "Ingrid, go to the hotel. I give you my word that the moment I have any information, I will *personally* call you."

Ingrid's eyes shut tightly, and more tears fall. I kiss them away, but more trail down her cheeks. "I'm sorry, sweetheart, I love you," are the only words I can manage before Pop stands between me and Ingrid.

"Commander," Pop barks out, "you're going to see the medical team before you see Ingrid again."

I raise my chin, but can't muster a salute. "Yes, Sir."

Though I can't see her, I hear the small admission, "I love you, Cay. *We* love you," before two men attempt to steal me away from her. They'll deem me unfit to leave if I fight, so I try my hardest to remain as calm as possible.

"You're my everything, Ingrid," I shout, but then I grip Pop by the arm as he walks me a few steps away from her. "Pop, there's a journal. Please make sure it gets to Ingrid if things…"

"A true Rogers," he attempts to make light of it. "I'm not leaving your side, but I'll make sure she gets it."

"Sir, you can't join Rogers. You'll need to stay here."

Pop glances at their insignia. "Lieutenant, thank you for your concern, but as a retired Vice Admiral, I'm going to need you to put me in contact with your superiors if we have an issue here. My son is experiencing severe anxiety, and the last thing you need to do is isolate him. Wherever he goes, I go."

The men who pulled me from the one person who keeps my mind quiet glance at each other and nod. "Yes, Sir."

They lead Pop and me into a cold, sterile room with a metal table and two chairs. Just like the room I saw Ingrid, Pop, and Cass in, there's a one-way mirror. This isn't a mental health screening. It's a fucking interrogation.

My jaw tics, wondering how much masking this will take to get back to Ingrid and our baby—though even I can see the possession over her and our child's safety is extreme.

"Be honest with them, but… you need to rein it in, son."

Pop is right. If I don't get a hold of what I'm feeling right now, they'll never let me see my girl again.

*Fuck!*

All it took was a fucking plane rattling our building. But, so help me, if anything or anyone hurts Ingrid or our child…

"Rogers." Pop's voice snaps my attention to him. "This is Doctor Franz. She'll be evaluating you today."

*Did she introduce herself? Was I daydreaming? I need to get my shit together.*

"Commander Rogers, it's a pleasure to meet you. It's my understanding you may need someone to talk to."

"Where's Ingrid?" I growl.

"Ingrid?"

"His wife," Pop finishes, his tone still gruff. I'm not delusional. I know Ingrid isn't my wife, but I still appreciate the gesture.

"Your wife is doing great." *She's so full of shit.* "Let's start with how you're feeling."

"You can all stop placating me," I groan. "I know Ingrid isn't my wife, as much as I want her to be. I don't know what happened in that hall. But the woman I love is worried about me."

"I see," she replies, noting something in my chart.

"Don't 'I see' me! Ingrid is the one thing that has kept me sane when I was stuck on that fucking boat for months. I passed the psych screenings. For a moment, I was worried about the safety of Ingrid and our child. It passed."

"I see," she repeats.

A growl rumbles in my chest, but Pop covers my hand in warning to quiet me. When I quickly glance over, he shakes his head once.

This looks bad.

"Does Ingrid not want to see me?"

"No one said that," she replies.

*Oh, for fuck's sake.*

Fear overcomes me. My only hope is that they'll deem me sane enough to see Ingrid and our baby girl again. Before I can say anything, Pop asks, "When can Ingrid see him?"

"He can see her now. Is she local?"

"I'm sure she's made a name for herself arguing with every officer between here and our rental car," Pop laughs. "I'm confident you'll be able to find her quick enough."

Seventeen minutes later, Cass and Ingrid enter the room. I stand at the sight of her. Both of their eyes widen—to be fair, this probably wasn't what they expected to be walking in on.

"Now that your sister and wife are—"

"I'm not sure why I'm here. Cay is my brother, but let's be honest, in what world would sibling data be relevant in a report." Ingrid pinches Cass. *"Ouch!* What?"

My beautiful and very pregnant Ingrid approaches the doctor. "He's not my husband. Not sure whether he disclosed that, but he isn't. That doesn't mean that he's not mine."

The doctor looks between Ingrid and me, and it takes every ounce of me not to pull her onto my lap in front of everyone. I *am* hers. I always have been.

"What did they tell you before you came in?" Pop asks Cass and Ingrid.

"This doesn't follow protocol," the doctor interjects, adjusting her glasses.

"No offense, but since your mental healthcare—*and, well, your health system in general*—is broken, can I take Cay home and call if we need assistance?" Ingrid's tone is full of anger she's trying to contain. But her fighting for this has me at a crossroads between being even more in love with her and staying to get help. I can't risk accidentally harming her if I have another episode. "I'm just a civilian, but the man I love is hurting. I think he just needs a night with his family."

The doctor sees exactly what Ingrid is up to and isn't convinced. Pop adds, "Commander Rogers is experiencing what appears to be a PTSD response to a plane that shook the building. He's not a current threat to himself, Ingrid, or their child. As soon as we get him home, we'll ensure he sees appropriate medical and military personnel prior to his six months of shore duty."

Giving her personal contact information and reminding Ingrid of the emergency services numbers, the doctor reluctantly releases me. After my episode, I'm genuinely surprised, especially when we're out of earshot and Ingrid tells me, "You're not broken, Cay. We're going to figure this out."

"What did they tell you?"

"It doesn't matter."

I swallow hard. "And what about you and me?"

"We need to start over, like we agreed. But that doesn't mean I love you any less. We're going to get you whatever help you need, together."

# ingrid

. . .

Caleb and I step into the hotel room, unsure of how the other is about to respond. I set my bag down on the small table and he offers, "I'll take the couch."

"Cay…"

"No, it's okay. I need you and the baby to feel safe. I can't protect you if we stay the night together."

It's only five-thirty. I'm not remotely tired… *Well, that's a lie. I'm always tired.* But I couldn't sleep no matter how much I might want to. I take Caleb's hand and drag him into the other room. "Lay down." Cay does as I ask, and I lay on the bed next to him. "See, everyone is okay."

I wrap my arms around him and take a deep breath. "Until I hurt you." His eyes shut tightly, and so does his hold on me.

As I lift my leg to pull his between mine, we're a little pretzel. "You'd never hurt me, or our baby, Cay."

Nuzzling into his chest, he sighs against me, muttering phrases like, "I don't deserve you," and "You're too good for me." I ignore all of it, refusing to give in to the lies.

After several minutes, I've had enough. "Cay, stop, please."

"What if it happens again? I could've hurt you today."

"Look at me." I drag his gaze to me. "You never hurt me, or our baby. I know you love us" He kisses my neck, then drags his lips back to mine. "We'll start over the moment we're home. We'll talk about all the hard things. Right now, it's just you and me, okay?"

"Can I touch you?" My heart breaks in two at his question. Pain must be marring my face because he quickly adds, "I didn't mean it like that."

"That's not why I'm here. I missed you, but... I'm huge, Cay." My hormones have gone haywire these past few weeks, and there's absolutely no way I'll admit to him that I touch myself every night to relieve the ache.

He pulls me closer until our bodies are melding as one. "You're beautiful. I don't need to be inside you, I just need to hold you."

Even after today, I don't fear him like he thinks. I nestle closer and wrap my arms tighter around his middle, no matter how uncomfortable my bra is. After being in his arms for a while, he settles his hand on the middle of my back, and he scratches where my clasp usually is.

"I've had to swap to a nursing bra," I laugh. "I've been leaking already."

Cay chuckles then glances down. "Fuck, you're still wearing that sexy dress from earlier." He sits upright and rushes out, "Do you want to change? Can I get you comfortable pants, a shirt, your favorite bra…"

"No, I'll get it," I laugh. "One sec." I get up and change into a pair of comfortable boy-shorts and one of his tees. The moment I slip on the shirt, a rumble comes from his chest. "Don't you dare pretend that this is attractive." I slide into bed next to him. Caleb takes off his pants and shirt, tossing them to the floor. His body is significantly more toned than I remember. "There isn't an ounce of body fat on you. How is that fair?"

"You stripped down to show off your perfect body that I've been missing for months. You're right, pretty sure I'm getting the better deal here."

"You pronounced 'whale' wrong."

"Don't talk about my wife that way."

"Cay," I say carefully, "you know I'm not your wife, right?"

"I know." He sighs, wraps me tightly in his arms, and admits, "For now."

Even if he's right, this feels exactly like it did when I arrived in Sapphire Lake. Neither of us are going to take our time; Caleb is inevitable. I can try to fight this, but one day he's going to slip a ring on my finger… and the thought no longer scares me.

# caleb

. . .

After a short nap, I wake to the sound of the shower. It takes me a second to put together where I am, but soft moans echo from the bathroom. I abruptly sit up, knowing damn well what she's doing.

Sliding out of bed, I follow the sweet gasps, finding the outline of Ingrid bracing herself against the wall with her other hand between her legs. I push open the shower door, making her jump.

"Cay!" she squeaks. "You're awake." My eyes fall to her hand barely covering her pussy, and she quickly pulls it away. "It's not what it looks like."

"Fuck, you're beautiful." I slip off my boxer briefs and step into the shower, my gaze never leaving hers as the steam surrounds us. Brushing the wet hair off her shoulder, I press a gentle kiss to the crook of her neck, and a whimper passes her lips.

"I missed you." Her breath is broken as her fingers rake through my hair.

"Did you finish?"

"No," she sheepishly whispers. "But"—I swipe the pad of my thumb over her peaked nipple, making her gasp—"you don't have to."

I graze my teeth against the side of her neck. "Do you want me to?"

"Please." Her breathless beg will forever be my undoing.

Peppering sweet kisses up her neck, I whisper, "Tell me you're mine, Ingrid." While I've loved her my whole life, now that I have her, I'm deathly afraid of losing her. I need to hear it.

She cups my face and brings my lips to hers. Her tongue teasing, begging for entry as I graze my knuckle against her clit, eliciting a moan from her. "I'm yours, but—"

I slip a finger inside her, and, *fuck*, she's tight. "But what?"

"Please don't rush this."

"There's no three-minute timer," I chuckle. "I'll happily taste and touch you for hours."

Ingrid rests her forehead on my chest and takes a deep breath. "That's not what I meant."

"I know." Curling my finger inside her, I tease her clit with my thumb. It's not enough, I have to taste her. "I'm going to take care of you, and once you come for me, I'm spending the rest of the night with you in my arms while you tell me everything that has happened since I left."

I drop to my knees and spread her legs, pressing a kiss to her belly. I missed so much in such a short time, the need to make up for it overcomes me. Moving lower, I add a finger and lick small firm circles around her clit.

"Cay," she breathes, bucking against my mouth, and I fucking love it; unable to get enough. As I continue playing, her nails dig into my scalp, pulling me closer. "Fuck, keep doing that, I'm close."

I'll happily remain on my knees for her until she shatters for me, but it doesn't take long before her legs begin to shake. I'm worried she could lose her balance so I pull back and stand, keeping my fingers inside her, not letting up. Roughly kissing her, I mutter against her lips, "You're incredible, Ingrid. So fucking beautiful. I missed touching you like this. Let go, come for me."

Ingrid grips me tightly as she coats my fingers, moaning my name as she rides out her orgasm. I've craved her clenching around my fingers like this, so much so that my cock is leaking.

"You're mine, princess. You're going to give me one more." I bring my fingers to my lips, sucking them clean. "Fuck, you taste amazing. Turn around, hands on the wall." She does as I ask, and I rub the head of my cock up and down her slick entrance, reminding her, "This ends the moment you want it to. I'll still be yours."

Ingrid pushes her ass closer, making me slip inside her tight, wet pussy. She looks over her shoulder, and I tilt her chin enough to capture her lips with mine. Our tongues dual for the upper hand, until she pulls back long enough to demand, "Say it again."

"I'm yours, Ingrid," I moan into her mouth as I slowly rock in and out of her. She feels too fucking good, I'm worried I won't last. Remaining deep inside her, I roll my hips to keep my thrusts short, memorizing how amazing she feels wrapped around me. The last time I was inside her is a distant memory, this time I want her branded on every inch of me.

My hand slides over one of hers, interlacing our fingers, and she rests her head against me. I take a moment to catalog every sense, wanting to commit it to my memory. If I could help it, I'd never spend a single day or night away from her ever again.

Her breathing becomes uneven, her gasps and moans louder. She tightens around me, and it's too much. Unable to hold on any longer, I thrust deep and paint the inside of her pussy with my release. As my cock twitches inside her, I reach around and circle her clit.

"I told you one more," I groan as she clenches tighter around me. "Give me one more."

Sucking on her neck to replace the mark I left last time, she screams out my name. It's fucking music. Her pussy pulses around my cock, and I don't want it to end.

Unfortunately, there is pounding on the shower door. "Was that a sex scream, or…?" Cass calls anxiously from the other side. While I felt better having the adjoining rooms unlocked, I'm now regretting it.

"I'm okay," Ingrid chuckles, though I make no move to pull out of her. The steam masks us enough that I don't need to worry about Cass or Pop seeing anything.

"Please get out," I groan.

"Fine, just keep it down next time."

Cass leaves, and Ingrid lets out a full laugh. As much as I shouldn't ignore what happened to me in that hallway today, I take the moment to pretend it didn't and appreciate the goddess before me. I kiss her shoulder and whisper, "Next time, I want the whole fucking hotel to hear you scream my name."

# ingrid

. . .

"Babe, why are you crying?" Cass rubs my back, but it does little to help calm me.

"It's too much."

"Shh, it's okay. Can I do anything to help?"

I blow my nose and wipe my eyes. "No, I'm just over-whelmed. I'm supposed to be on set in a few weeks, I'm tired all the fucking time, I need to find help for Caleb so I'm not on edge waiting for him to have an episode. Shit, he's only been home for a few days! I miss Smitten, and I'm pretty sure Cay is going to propose, and I don't know if I'm ready. I'm hungry… and horny. Everything sucks."

Cassidy wraps me in a tight hug and laughs, "I'm not going to fuck you, but I can get you a snack!" I sniffle and wipe my nose on her sweater. "And I'll happily be your tissue. It's going to be fine. Amanda and the director love the script, so there's nothing to worry about there. As far as Cay is concerned, we'll make sure he sees a therapist, and if they need him to be on medication, we'll get him that, too. There's a solution for everything you're mentioning, but I think you're trying to fix it all by yourself."

"I don't want to burden you," I admit softly.

She pulls back and grabs my shoulders. "Now, you listen to me, none of this is a burden. With you needing to be in LA in a few weeks, do you want to come back home, or just look for a place here and stay?"

"I know Cay will want to go back home."

"That's not what I asked. What do *you* want? He's in love with you and would move to the moon if you asked him to."

"I know," I laugh and blow my nose, "that's what I'm afraid of."

Cass gets up to grab her tablet, already swiping as she sits back down. "Okay, where do you want to live?"

"Cay will need to stay close to base."

"But…?"

My shoulders fall. "I don't want to drive hours to work every day."

"What if you get an apartment near the set, and then just come see Cay on the weekends?"

"He'll hate that." I shake my head. "No, I need to suck it up and commute."

"It's six months, *he* can suck it up."

Rubbing my belly, I sigh, "This little one will be here soon, he's going to miss the first few months with her."

"Military babies are used to it." She shrugs. "Cay and I didn't see Pop for months at a time. I don't remember being three months old, your little girl won't either."

"Gah, I hate this!"

"Let's find you a dog-friendly apartment. Big enough that Travis or I can come visit and not have to stay on the couch." Swiping through the listings she gasps, finding a larger three-bedroom condo that has a beautiful outdoor space with fake grass for Smitten. "It's in Santa Monica, not too far from the studio. Plus, you'll be close to the water. I have a feeling your little Aquarius baby will love the beach."

"What about...?"

"Cay will be fine. Just have him stay on base. He'll be able to take leave, since he's just running trainings. Pop said it's in his contract that he gets at minimum two weekends a month, but I'm sure he'll be able to take more." She laughs to herself, shaking her head. "When I say it out loud, he does kind of sound like a divorced dad with custody every other weekend. But all of it is temporary! I'll see if I can take a month off when the baby is born and come help you get everything settled."

"Are you sure? I don't want to be—"

"You're my best friend. I'm going to be here when my niece is born." Her eyes soft, she adds, "We're family. Now, let's set up a tour with the property manager and get you this perfect little home."

# caleb

. . .

"It's perfect," I whisper, wrapping my arms around Ingrid from behind. She jumps at first but exhales a sigh of relief, placing her hands on top of mine as our baby kicks against them. *Fuck, I'm going to miss this.*

"You don't mind that I'll be hours away?"

"We'll make it work. It's just for six months." The only way she'd be able to stay with me is if we got married. I've only been back for a few days; proposing is out of the question. She's not ready, though I'd marry her today if she were.

The property manager chimes in, "There is a six-hundred dollar pet deposit. First and last month's rent—puts you at $21,800."

I sputter a cough. "$21,800?"

"You should see New York City rent," Ingrid laughs. "We'll take it."

"When would you like to move in?"

"Today?" Ingrid asks hopefully.

"If only we could move that quickly. I'll need to run your credit check and contact your references, but if everything clears, I can have you in here in two days."

Ingrid beams, and as much as I'll hate that she's here by herself, the condo is perfect. We have an ocean view, and I can picture us barbecuing on the rooftop deck in the spring. Smitten will have plenty of space, too.

After Ingrid hands over our application, we walk out to the rental car. As soon as the property manager is out of earshot, I ask, "Are you sure about this? Ten-thousand a month is pretty steep. I know we haven't talked about finances much—or at all, really—but that's about what I make in a month. It doesn't exactly leave room for anything else."

Open the car door for her, she lifts onto her toes to kiss my cheek before getting in. "Lucky for you, I'm not unemployed."

I keep my hand in hers for the two hour drive back to San Diego. Neither of us say much, but truly, I don't know what to say. Having to bide my time and not rush this with her is going to be harder than any military training I've gone through.

Ingrid rests her head on my shoulder and closes her eyes. Even though the wait will be torture, she's worth it, our baby is worth it. At a stop light, I kiss the top of her head and whisper, "I love you."

A few moments later, she sleepily sighs, "I love you, too."

"We got the place!" Ingrid squeals, and I don't remember the last time she was this excited. That thought alone upsets me.

"That was fast. When can you move in?" It only took them twenty-four hours to process the application. I'm hoping we can move in sooner rather than later so I can help get everything ready for Ingrid and the baby before I'm due on base.

"Excuse me, mister." She places her hands on her hips. "Your name is on the rental agreement, too."

"It's your place, Ingrid," I laugh.

Her eyes narrow. "So, you're allowed to get a dog that's *ours*, but I'm not allowed to get a condo that's *ours?*"

"Fuck, you're adorable. Come here."

Ingrid joins me on the couch, but I pat my lap. "Not a chance."

"Don't make me ask again."

"Technically, you didn't ask." I pull her onto my lap to straddle me, making her giggle. "Do you ever not get your way, Commander Rogers?"

"Fuck, I love when you call me that." She leans in and kisses me, the smile never leaving her lips. Sliding my hand into her hair, I angle her to deepen our kiss. I'll never get enough of her. Our daughter kicks, and I feel it against my torso. "She's been feisty lately."

"Wonder where she got that from?"

I break our kiss long enough to ask, "Have you thought about names?"

"I have."

"And?"

She bites her lip. "Darcy."

"It's perfect."

"Isn't it? I feel like she's going to be a sassy one; it fits. Darcy Elizabeth Rogers."

My heart stops and I swallow hard. "She'll have my last name?"

Ingrid's smile widens. "I will, too. *One day*. Or have you changed your mind about that?"

"Don't you dare joke about that, princess."

"Oh no, princess is back!" I lay Ingrid on the couch, and she bursts into laughter. "Come on, Cay, we don't have time for that."

"There's always time for a quick breakfast."

# ingrid

. . .

Six Weeks Later

"Quiet on set," Penelope, the director, announces.

I've been on my feet for ten hours today, and I'm moments away from falling asleep standing. While my doctor says I can have two cups of coffee a day, I'm to the point of needing the stuff they give truckers to stay up all night. A little gas station speed would be amazing right about now. Darcy has been more active lately, and I'm just hoping to make it a couple more weeks.

"Ingrid," Amanda whispers. "You might want to go to the bathroom."

"Oh, I'm fine. I'll go after we finish the scene."

"Trust me."

Following their gaze, I look down and my pants have a wet spot, looking a hell of a lot like I peed myself. I cover myself with my hands. "Shit! This is so embarrassing. I've been standing for so long, my legs must be numb." I rush off to the bathroom and stop right outside the set doors when my legs feel cold. Looking down again, my pants are now soaked.

*Did my water break?*

A woman from craft services has a rolling cart and sees the light glow above me that filming has started. She waits, but when she sees what I'm dealing with, she gasps. "Do you need me to call someone?"

"Yes," I groan as pain suddenly radiates through my lower back. My phone is still in my purse, which is inside. "My bag is in there. Can you call for a cab or something? Maybe by the time they are here I can get my purse."

"What does it look like?"

"Navy blue, canvas material."

She takes out her phone and texts someone. "Okay, Kim is inside and looking for it. She can bring it to the door."

A few minutes and another contraction later, a woman swiftly opens the door and hands me the bag. I mouth "thank you" and quickly take out my phone. I text Cass, Cay, and Pop in a single message.

> I think my water broke. Going to the hospital. I'll text you when I get there.

CASSIDY

> Pop and I will be on the next flight!

> Don't, it's okay. It might be a false alarm.

> Fine, I'll be on the next flight and Pop will come when you know for sure.

> Couldn't wait two weeks for me?

Cay doesn't reply but he could be leading a training session right now. I'm about to order a rideshare when the door opens again, and Amanda appears. "Shit! Is that what I think it is?"

"Maybe," I wince. "I'm sorry!"

"No, it's fine. Is there someone to take you to the hospital?"

I shake my head. "I'm just going to order a—"

"Jack is on his way since we were almost done for the day. He was going to take me to dinner; I'll call him." She pulls out her phone and dials. "Hey, Ingrid needs a ride to the hospital. How far out are you?... Perfect, can you pull up to lot eight?... Yep, that's the one. Thank you, I love you." Hanging up, she then tells me, "He's less than three minutes out."

"Are you sure about this?"

Amanda glances up and down the hallway muttering something about a medical drama. She rushes down to another set and comes back running with a wheelchair. "They stole my bloody knives for our flashback scene. I'm stealing their wheelchair."

I don't protest and let her wheel me to the car. When we get through the double doors, a dark gray SUV is waiting for us. The man driving has his hair tied up in a messy bun, wearing a white button-down shirt that has the top buttons undone, suspenders, and dress slacks. As much as Amanda has told me about Jack, this is not at all how I pictured him.

He gets out to open the door and offers his hand to help me in. "Is the wee bairn joining us today?"

"I hope not," I whine.

Once he closes the door, he rounds the car and gets in, then rolls the window down. "Spitfire," he calls, and she moves closer to the car. "As soon as you're done filming, we're still going for drinks and dinner. Don't think you can get out of celebrating our anniversary."

"It's not our anniversary," she deadpans.

"It's not?"

"No, it's next week!"

"*Shite*. Are you sure?"

"Yes!" Amanda laughs. "Now, get her to the hospital."

Jack rolls up the window, and the whole drive he reminds me to breathe. His voice is extremely calming, but I'll give credit to his thick Scottish accent. If he narrated audiobooks, I'd listen to all of them.

We pull up to the hospital, and he helps me get checked in. "Are you sure you don't want me to wait with you? Amanda won't mind."

"It's okay, thank you again for driving me. I'm sorry if I ruined your car." I grimace, but he chuckles.

"It's fine, do you need me to call someone?"

"I'm trying to get a hold of Caleb, but the reception is bad here. Would you mind calling him for me when you're on the road?"

"Of course." He nods, and I send him Caleb's number.

"Shit! My dog! She's still at the house."

"What kind?"

"A Dalmatian."

"Christ, woman!" He lets out a hearty laugh. "It'll eat everything in sight. Give me your key, and I'll take it for a walk while you're here. If you need anything else, Amanda and I will be close by."

"You're amazing! Thank you so much."

He leaves, and a few minutes later, a woman wheels me back into a triage room and does a swab for amniotic fluid. Turns out, my water did indeed break, and she insists I won't be leaving until my baby is born. I groan, laying my head further into the pillow. The timing couldn't be worse.

# caleb

. . .

On my way to my therapy appointment, I get a call from an international number I don't recognize. I send it to voicemail, and once the alert lights up on my phone, I click on it. A Scottish man's voice comes through the car speakers.

*"Caleb. This is Jack. You don't know me, but Ingrid works with my wife, Amanda, and she told me to call you. I just dropped her off at the hospital. She gave me her key—"*

I don't listen to the rest of the message and call him back. He picks up on the second ring.

"This is Jack."

"How is she?" I rush out.

"Caleb?"

"Yes, where's Ingrid?"

"Rest assured, your lass is fine."

"She's not hurt?" I gulp.

"Not at all," he laughs. "Her water broke on set, so I drove her to the hospital. Did you not listen to my message?"

"No," I sigh. "Sorry, I just heard she was in the hospital and called you back."

"Your wife is doing great. Her contractions slowed on the drive over."

"She's in labor?" I ask a little too loudly. I don't bother correcting that she's not my wife.

"Aye. She gave me her key to take your dog for a walk, so you can go straight to the hospital."

I glance at the clock, and I'll be hitting traffic; might take me close to three hours. "I'm on my way. Thank you for taking her."

We hang up, and he texts me the address. I pull over to type it into the GPS when I notice missed texts and calls from Ingrid, Cass, and Pop.

*Shit!*

Cass is heading to the airport, Pop is going to stay behind a day or two in case it's a false alarm, and as I'm scrolling the messages, a call comes in from a Los Angeles area code. It could be Ingrid, so I answer.

"Ingrid?" I can't mask my worry.

"Hey. I can't call from my cell, the reception is trash here. My water broke. Can you come?"

"I already signed out for the weekend. I was headed to my therapy appointment when I got the call. I planned on surprising you by driving up tonight." There's a guttural, feral moan, and I hear a woman in the background walking her through deep breathing. "I'm on my way."

We hang up, and I leave a message for my therapist that I'll be missing my appointment today. The drive takes me just shy of three hours to get to the hospital, but it feels longer than the six months I was away from Ingrid. I haven't received another call, so my hope is that I didn't miss her giving birth.

Pulling up to the hospital, I park in a visitor spot and practically sprint through the front doors. After checking in at reception, a nurse walks me back into one of the labor and delivery rooms. Ingrid is resting, and I lean against the doorframe, hands in my pockets, admiring the most beautiful woman I've ever known.

Ingrid must sense my presence because her eyes flutter open, and she mutters, "What next? Backward ball cap? Or do you have gray sweatpants hiding somewhere?"

"Hey, princess." I push off the doorframe and take a seat next to her bed. "How are you feeling?" Taking one of her hands in both of mine, I bring her knuckles to my lips.

"Hungry."

"Fuck, I love you," I laugh, leaning in to kiss her forehead. Small beads of sweat dust her hairline; she must be fucking exhausted.

Suddenly, she gasps, almost doubling over and gripping her belly. A moment later, a nurse comes in and tells Ingrid, "As soon as this contraction passes, I'm going to see how much you've dilated."

The nurse checks a few things and does a quick ultrasound but doesn't say anything. Finally, she tells us she's going to get the doctor, who comes in a few minutes later.

Her doctor presses her glasses up the bridge of her nose. "I know you wanted to deliver vaginally, but with where the baby is positioned, we may need to consider a cesarean instead."

"No," Ingrid groans through her pain, shaking her head. "We had a plan."

"For the health of the baby, we can let you push a few times, but if she doesn't change positions, it may be our only option," the doctor insists.

"Ingrid," I say softly, "when has anything ever gone to plan for us? It's okay if we bring our daughter into this world a different way than you wanted to. We need to make sure you and Darcy are safe."

"Last resort," she demands.

"Last resort," I echo, brushing a few damp strands of hair off her forehead. "You're doing amazing. Everything is going to be fine."

# ingrid

. . .

" $S$ he's perfect," Cass coos, snuggling Darcy.

*Darcy is more than perfect, she's the most beautiful creature on the fucking planet.*

I can't even enjoy my daughter's light dusting of strawberry blonde hair, or the adorable sigh she has. I'm in so much pain after the cesarean; mostly from gas, but the doctors claim I can't be given anything for it except a damn mint. Cay has snapped at the nurses for not listening, so I'm sure we're on a shit list until we're discharged. I'm moments away from begging Caleb to run to the store to buy simethicone over the counter.

There's a soft knock at the door before Pop walks in. "Hey, kiddo, how are you feeling?"

"I'm great," Cassidy jests and Pop rolls his eyes. He moves further into the room, and Cass passes Darcy to him. "She's adorable, isn't she?"

Pop's voice is strained when he finally answers, "You guys did good."

He begins to hand her off to me, but I insist, "It's Caleb's turn."

Caleb takes her, whispering something to our sweet baby girl. With Cay still having a few months of duty, I want him to have as much time with her as possible. I don't know that I've ever seen him this happy. Ever since he got back, he's been on edge, waiting for another episode to hit. His doctors have him on two different medications to hopefully help with it, but today is the first day I've seen his wide smile in a long fucking time. Now if only he was able to grow out his beard…

I sit up, wincing with pain in my abdomen and my pussy. Trying to push in attempt to have a vaginal delivery was fucking stupid—after the c-section, now everything hurts. Caleb's smile fades, replaced with worry etched on all of his features. I swipe my thumb between his brows, and his frown softens.

Cass chimes in, "Is it local to the incision?"

"No," I grit out. "It's like I have really bad"—I lower my voice so hopefully only she can hear—"gas."

Cass barks a laugh. "Give me ten minutes. There's a little gift shop that has some over-the-counter medication." Without a chance to protest, she rushes out of the room.

Pop offers, "Can I get either of you something from the cafeteria?"

"Would you mind getting me a coffee?" Caleb asks, then quickly turns his attention to me. "What do you need?"

"I'm okay," I chuckle. "Thank you."

As soon as Pop leaves, I take Darcy and lay her on my chest. Caleb's smile returns and reaches into his pocket. "I know this is probably the worst time to ask—"

"Don't," I yelp. "Cay, I love you, but today is Darcy's day. We'll have ours."

Caleb leans over me and kisses my temple; I hum in response. Little Darcy makes an adorable whimpered sigh and every worry I had that Cay and I would be shitty parents is thrown out the window. It's going to be a rough few months, but Cass will help me for some of it, and Caleb will be here as much as he can until his six months are up.

We're going to be okay.

"I love you, princess." He kisses me softly, and I sigh against his lips, but my phone lighting up in the corner of my eye pulls my attention from him.

"It might be Amanda."

"I don't think she's going to ask you to come into work today," he laughs, handing me my phone.

It isn't a message, it's a news alert.

### Martin Harris Fired for Alleged Sexual Misconduct

A shiver cascades down my limbs and my throat is dry. "Cay…"

"What is— *Oh*. That." His jaw tics, but a small smirk appears.

I eye him suspiciously. "Did you know about this?"

"Sort of. I had to slay the dragon, but he deserves more than being fired."

"Cay," I screech, but it stirs Darcy. I lower my voice to a whisper-shout. "Cay, what did you do?"

He blows out a long breath and rubs the back of his neck. "I was talking to my therapist one day, and it hit me that when you confessed what happened to you, we were being watched. I asked about who heard it, and they couldn't do anything because it wasn't an official statement from you." He pauses before continuing, "I knew you weren't the first, so I checked with a few intelligence people I know to look into it. Apparently, there was a woman who made an official police statement, but it was brushed under the rug."

"So, how is it public?"

"I'm not sure. That's where my dragon slaying ended. I realized that it could drag you and our baby into it, so I asked that both of us be left out of any reports."

*No other woman will have to deal with his tiny cock again... unless she's into that.*

"You did that?" I breathe.

He huffs a small laugh. "Yeah, I did that. It was on my bucket list."

"And what else is on your bucket list?" I tease.

He brushes a soft kiss to my lips. "I told you, it begins and ends with you."

# caleb

...

Five Months Later

I wake up in a mild panic that Ingrid isn't next to me and Darcy isn't in her crib beside our bed. The faint sound of a blender in the kitchen has my heart slowing. I rush out of bed and put on sweatpants and a tee before making my way downstairs. As I reach the kitchen, I'm finally able to take a full breath when I find Ingrid on the couch, nursing Darcy on one side and using a breast pump on the other. On the table is a green smoothie that doesn't look like it's been touched. I feel... *helpless*. There's nothing I can do for her in this moment.

Moving her smoothie to the side, I take a seat on the coffee table and prop Ingrid's feet on my lap. "You should've woken me up."

Ingrid sighs a moan as I massage her feet. "You're going to have her all day, I needed to get everything ready." My jaw tics; she didn't need to do anything.

"Did you pack yourself lunch?"

"Not yet."

I move her feet off my lap and press a kiss to both her and Darcy's foreheads. Ingrid attempts to protest, but I'm already up and headed for the kitchen. After washing my hands, I portion out leftover pasta bolognese from last night and sprinkle entirely too much parmesan on top. While I prefer a light dusting, hers is always more cheese than pasta. I cap the leftovers' container and search for a lid that will fit the small container for her.

*Why can I never find the right one?*

After looking for several minutes, I give up and find another container that has a lid that fits. Then, I wash an apple and put it in her lunchbox with a cold pack. Her breast pump turns off, and I glance up—Darcy is still nursing, and Ingrid is struggling to top the bottle. I'm at her side in an instant. Once it's sealed, I place it in the fridge and take apart the pieces of her breast pump attachment, wash them, and put them in the countertop sterilizer. I've only been here a few days, and it's a stab in the gut that I haven't been here the whole time to help her. I'm already exhausted, and I've done nothing. She's been doing this on her own since Darcy was born; I've missed almost all of it.

Smitten comes barreling in, and Darcy pulls away from Ingrid at the sound, milk squirting onto Ingrid's clothes and onto Darcy.

"Fuck." I take Darcy from her, and Darcy lets out an adorable giggle. "You think that was funny?"

Ingrid chuckles, "Welcome to the shitshow, Cay."

I get Darcy cleaned up while Ingrid changes her clothes. I take a seat on the couch with Darcy and we open up a board book for me to read to her. Smitten paws at me and I give her a teasing glare. "Are you going to be a good girl for me today?"

"Oh, I'm absolutely going to be a good fucking girl," Ingrid laughs from behind me.

"Get over here."

Ingrid bites her lip and circles the couch to kiss me goodbye. The moment the front door closes, Darcy lets out an obnoxious fart that ends in a gurgling sound. With a deep sigh, I take her to the bedroom to change her. Sure enough, there's an explosion of epic proportions to clean up. It runs out of the diaper, and despite me yelling, "No, no no," it ends up on the comforter anyway. *Fuck! I forgot the changing pad!* Not sure why I thought yelling at a diaper would help, but lesson learned: It does not.

I finish getting Darcy cleaned up and place her in the crib to strip the bed. I put the comforter in the washing machine, only to find we are out of laundry soap. I grab my keys to make a quick trip to the store when Smitten barks at me.

"What?" She growls and tugs at my sweatpants. "Oh, right, might not want to go out in these."

I return to the bedroom to change to find Darcy crying. "Fuck, shit... I mean, *shoot*. I didn't forget you, sweetheart." Picking her up, guilt overcomes me. I absolutely did forget her, and she fucking knows it.

Definitely not winning 'Dad of the Year' over here.

"Let's go for a ride." Smitten's ears perk up. "No, not you, pup. I'll be back in a bit."

I change into jeans, and Darcy and I head to the store. She's just starting to sit up properly, and I don't want to risk her toppling over in a shopping cart. Rummaging in the truck for the baby carrier so I can wear her, I find it beneath one of the seats. After getting her strapped in, we head into the store.

Darcy and I only make it down one aisle when a woman coos, "Oh, look at you. You're such a great dad!"

*What the fuck?*

"Uh, yeah... thanks..." I'm not a great dad, I almost left our daughter at the house!

It happens three more times before we make it to the laundry detergent that I nearly forgot with all the distractions. I swear one woman was trying to flirt with me, but seeing as I don't have a wedding ring, I can't fault her for trying. Another said it was so great seeing a dad watching their own child. Honestly, I took offense to it. I'm not Darcy's babysitter; she's my daughter, for fuck's sake.

Oh, the stories I'll have for Ingrid later.

Darcy and I leave with detergent, beef jerky for me, puff snacks for Darcy, and dog treats for Smitten. As soon as we're home, I breathe a sigh of relief that the worst of today is over...

*What is that?*

Ingrid's underwear is torn to ribbons and strewn on the floor. Not just one pair... all of them.

"Smitten!" I yell into the house. Mid-chew, Smitten appears with a lacy black thong hanging out of her mouth.

"You are *not* a good girl." Darcy cries. "No, sweetheart, you're perfect. Smitten is an ass—*tronaut*."

I really need to watch my language around Darcy. The last thing I need is her first word to be 'fuck' or 'asshole.'

Placing Darcy in the playpen, I give her a kiss on the cheek, then scour the house for rogue, half-eaten panties. I don't know that I'll be able to replace them before Ingrid's home—she might have to go without tonight. I smile at the thought.

The rest of the morning and early afternoon is much smoother. With Darcy down for a nap, I take a few minutes to close my eyes, but it isn't restful. Every little noise she makes, or Smitten's tail thumping on the floor, keeps me from sleeping. Giving up, I make my way into the kitchen and pull out half a pound of ground beef from the fridge.

*What the fuck am I going to make for dinner?*

I check the cabinets and find a pack of hamburger buns; grilling it is. Taking out various spices and an egg, I prep patties for cheeseburgers when Ingrid gets home. As I'm putting them in the fridge, far away from Smitten, Darcy wakes from her nap over half an hour early. I get her changed—this time remembering the changing pad—and it's the reminder I needed that I forgot to start the laundry when we got home.

It's about time for Darcy to have a bottle, so I warm one from the fridge. The cap with the nipple isn't fitting properly, so I force it on, only for the entire bottle to spill on the counter. Bracing my hands on the edge of the counter, I hang my head in defeat and take a deep breath, then clean up the mess and prep another bottle.

Needing to get out of the cursed condo, once Darcy is done with her bottle, I take her and Smitten to the beach for a walk on the pier. When we reach the end, we look out onto the water and have a quick snack. Smitten tries to steal a fish a man caught, and thankfully, he is understanding. A little too understanding. While, yes, I have my hands full, I doubt Ingrid experiences this kind of grace regularly.

We take our time getting back to the condo, and I spot Ingrid's car parked out front. To say I'm relieved is an understatement. Once inside, I spot Ingrid pumping on the couch. She looks up and parts her lips as if she's about to say something, but her eyes widen.

"How was your day?" I set the keys on the counter and take a seat next to her, blowing out a long breath.

"Great... How was *your* day?"

"Fu—*dge*. It was... How the hell do you do this every day?" I recount everything that happened, and Ingrid laughs so hard she's crying. "I don't see how this is funny! Everything that could go wrong, did go wrong." Even though today was a mess, the chaos kept me present, and I wouldn't change that for anything.

"I'm sorry. You did good, Cay." She leans in and kisses me on the cheek. "Tomorrow will be easier, I promise."

"I'm locking all our clothes in a safe while you're at work."

"No need," she chuckles. "We wrapped early. They did the last scene this afternoon, and Amanda said she'll video call me if she needs anything." Her breast pump stops, and she replaces her pads into her bra, setting the pumped milk on the coffee table. Darcy reaches for her, so I quickly take the bottles and carefully cap them before placing them in the fridge. As I sit back down on the couch, she asks, "I was thinking... What do you think about moving back to Sapphire Lake?"

# ingrid

### . . .

## Two Months Later

S itting on our back porch, Darcy is snuggled against me as I rock her in the swing Pop installed last year. It feels like yesterday that I ran from New York to spend time with my best friend and her family, but with everything that's happened, it also feels like decades.

The cool air coming off the lake makes the warm August weather bearable as I watch Smitten chase after a honeybee she'll never catch. Darcy wakes up from her short nap and watches Smitten leaping through the backyard. Her small giggle is all it takes before Smitten comes running toward us. "Easy, girl." She comes to a screeching halt in front of us and sits. Darcy reaches for her and grabs her ears, Smitten licking Darcy's bare legs. "Come on, no one wants slobber, Smitts!" She's such a good pup around Darcy, always making sure she's happy.

"What is this?" Caleb's voice pulls Darcy's and my attention, and she reaches for him. He's holding up a journal— *my journal*.

"Shit! I mean, *shoot*. That, uh... that's nothing," I feign ignorance, but it's taken Caleb hours to find it, even though I set it on the bed this morning... after one last letter.

"Sure as hell doesn't look like nothing." He cocks an eyebrow, and I do my best to smother a smile.

Stuffing a hand in his pocket, my eyes fall to his gray sweatpants. "Cay," I warn.

"Yes, princess?"

"What are those?"

"Don't change the subject," he chuckles.

Not only is there the outline of his perfect cock, and a distinct bulge that's conveniently the size of a jewelry box. He probably doesn't think I notice, but he's had it on him for months. "Tell you what, why don't we go on the boat, and you can read the journal on the way to the dock."

"This isn't a journal, they are letters... to me."

"So, you were snooping?" I tease.

"Obviously."

We glare at each other in a small standoff. "Did you just ruin my grand gesture moment?"

"Maybe..."

"Caleb Rogers, what am I going to do with you?" Just like everything with us, nothing is going to plan.

"Well," he chuckles, waving it aloft, "according to this, you're going to marry me." He opens the last page and begins reciting, "Ingrid's Bucket List. This list isn't all-inclusive, but it'll have to do for now. One, let myself fall in love with Caleb." He looks up at me; that one is crossed off and so is the next one. "Two, move back to Sapphire Lake. Three, enjoy our daughter for the first year before returning to work." He narrows his eyes. "You just took on the Harriet Alexander adaptation."

"Shh, keep reading."

He shakes his head and continues, "Four, practice giving Darcy a baby brother or sister." Pausing, he bites his lip and laughs. "Five, marry the love of my life."

"Yep, that about sums it up. What do you say we take that boat ride now?" I stand and keep Darcy on my hip, but she keeps reaching for Cay. Rolling my eyes, I pass her to him. "But I need to get dressed first."

Cay lifts her in the air, making her giggle. "You have five minutes, or I'll undress you myself."

He takes Darcy into the garden and plucks a daffodil for her as I rush into the house. I slip on my white sundress that I wore the day we were on the boat before he left. When I walk out onto the porch, his eyes are molten.

"If we're going on the boat, we need Cass to watch Darcy," he growls.

"Keep it in your pants, Rogers. Speaking of, you should change out of those. It's too warm for sweats, even if you look delicious."

"Fine." He hands me Darcy and kisses the side of my neck. "I'll be out in a minute."

Several later, he comes out with dress slacks and a button-down shirt that he's rolling the sleeves of. I bite my lip at the sight. "Damn it, Cay! That's almost worse than the sweatpants." I set it out for him. It's my own damn fault.

We get Darcy into her car seat, and I text Cass.

It's time.

CASSIDY

Fuck, he took forever.

Okay, let's do this!

"Cass will meet us at the boat."

Cay hums with a nod and slides his hand into mine, bringing my knuckles to his lips. The drive is short, and as we park, I turn and face him. "Do you still want to marry me?"

"What kind of question is that?" he laughs. "I'd marry you today if you were ready." I look over at the boat, and Caleb follows my gaze. "What's going on?"

"Nothing!" I squeak. "Let's go."

"What about Cass?"

Like clockwork, Cass knocks on his window. "Hey, guys!"

I squeeze his hand tightly. "While I was meeting with Harriet Alexander, she mentioned her uncle used to be a wedding planner. So, on your boat is Harriet's uncle, Ethan. He's certified to officiate weddings and also planned a little party for us after. Travis will be here with Smitten any minute now. Pop and Cass are here. If you're ready to get married, we can do it right now."

"Are you serious?"

"I wouldn't joke about this. Cay, I left the letters out on purpose. I'm ready."

He takes a deep breath to hide a sob stuck in his throat. "You're ready?"

"*We're* ready." Cass gets Darcy out of her car seat, while Cay kisses me. "No more lying to government officials that I'm your wife."

He laughs against my lips. "Fuck, I love you."

"Come on, they're waiting for us."

We get out of the truck and walk hand-in-hand toward the boat. The sun is high enough to create beautiful sparkles on the water, reflecting on our faces as we make our way down the dock. Cay opens the small door for me to step in and whispers, "Are you sure?"

"Are *you* sure?"

He follows me onto the pontoon and takes me in his arms. "I would've married you the night you came back into town."

"Yeah, he would've," Cass chimes in, taking a seat, thankfully not on the chase that will forever be burned into my brain as a sex-chair.

Travis runs down the dock with Smitten and Inferno. "I'm here!"

Cassidy looks up and, if I'm not mistaken, is checking him out. Even I'll admit, Travis looks good in jeans and a tee, but there's something about a man in expertly fitted slacks and a crisp button-down.

Smitten and Inferno leap into the boat and Smitten takes a seat next to Cass—always wanting to be by Darcy's side. With Pop and Ethan already on the pontoon, I sit in the captain's chair and start the motor. Caleb comes up behind me, presses a chaste kiss to my neck, and says quietly beside my ear, "You're in my seat."

"It's fine, I can't crash the boat in the middle of the lake," I laugh, but Caleb's face goes white as he glances at Darcy and back to me. *Shit!* "Cay, I'm sorry, I didn't mean it. You can drive if you want."

He takes a deep breath. "No, it's okay. But once Travis and I untie the boat from the dock, I'm going to be right here beside you."

"Deal." I grip the front of his shirt and bring his lips to mine.

Cay and Travis get everything untied, and we make our way into the middle of the lake. The sun is still warm and bright; the perfect late afternoon on the water.

I turn off the engine, and Travis lowers the anchor. Ethan stands and takes out a few note cards. "Ready when you are," he chuckles, and Caleb and I stand in front of him. "We are gathered here today…"

Through Ethan's words, I whisper to Caleb, "You were my first, Cay… and I want you to be my last."

# epilogue — caleb

· · ·

## Three Years Later

"Cay, we have exactly fifty-five minutes until Sebastian is up from his nap, and then we have to pick up Darcy from preschool." Ingrid strips off her tank top and tosses it to the ground. "You wrecked my pussy last night, so you'll need to get creative."

I move over to the dresser and pull out our nylon rope. "If you're tied to our bed, I can do whatever the fuck I want, princess."

She sucks in a breath. "That's not fair. I'm sore!"

"That's okay, I'll kiss it better."

"Cay," she groans, "I meant that I'll give you a blowie, or you can put it in my ass."

"Who says I can't make you come on my tongue, then my cock, and I finish in your mouth or your ass?" I shrug, and she gapes at me, not finding it the least bit amusing. We read a book together where the man made the woman come ten times. I took it as a challenge, but Ingrid tapped out after eight last night.

She still owes me two more…

"That is the *last time* we buddy read a book together." She crosses her arms over her chest, her perfect breasts now spilling out of her bra. I salivate at the sight, needing to taste her, right fucking now.

I stalk over to her, throwing the rope onto the bed. Taking her face in my hands, I roughly kiss her, reaching to the middle of her back to free her of the pointless clothing. Her bra falls to the ground, and I waste no time twisting one of her nipples between my fingers. She gasps into my mouth as I pinch harder. Fifty-five minutes is plenty to still take my time with her.

Ingrid reaches between us and palms my cock through my pants. I'm not taking them off until she comes for me. I'll be gentle with her pussy, but I know she needs me to be rough everywhere else. Gripping her wrist, I pull it behind her back, and she nips my lip in response.

"You're getting greedy, wife. How are you going to sit for hours tomorrow at the Silver Globes, after I've marked that perfect ass of yours?"

"Fifty-three minutes, husband."

A growl rumbles in my chest at her calling me that, and it only makes her laugh harder. Not wanting to waste another moment, I wrap the rope around her wrists and tie it tight enough that she won't be able to get out of it on her own. Tossing her further onto the bed, I grip her leggings and tear them down, then press her knees to the mattress, spreading her wide for me.

"What the fuck is this?"

"I trimmed." She pulls her lips into her mouth to smother a smile.

"*Trimmed?* You're fucking hairless!"

"Is that a problem?"

My eyes narrow. "Should I 'trim' my beard?"

Hers widen. "No!"

I lick up her center, making her shudder, then swirl my tongue around her clit. She tries to grip the covers above her head and begins squirming. Gasping as I pull her legs wider, she finally relaxes against my hold. My beard scrapes against her as I lick and suck harder, wanting to send her over the edge quickly. Thankfully, it doesn't take long before my beard is soaked, and she's quivering beneath me. I'll never grow tired of the taste of her.

*One down, one to go...*

With a chaste kiss to the inside of her thigh, I stand and pull out a bottle of lube from our nightstand. I toss it onto the bed and move her further up to make room for me. She hasn't recovered from her orgasm, but I don't want her to. I strip down naked and climb onto the bed, kissing up her body until I've marked her hip, breasts, and neck. As I reach her lips, I slide my cock inside her cunt to coat myself. Her moans fill the room as I thrust in and out a few times but pull out.

"Fuck, why did you stop?" she groans, though it comes out more of a pant.

I squeeze a fair amount of lube into my hand and slide my fingers up and down her tight ass, then press the head of my cock inside. She hisses, and I finally reply, "Because, my beautiful wife. I want to watch you come with my cock buried in your ass and your pussy clenching around my fingers." There isn't a moment of hesitation as she pulls her legs up for me to push deeper. "*Fuck*, you take me so well. Do you want a toy or my fingers in this perfect cunt?"

"Cay!" she squeals in embarrassment.

"Toy or fingers?" I grunt, my cock pressed in to the hilt.

"Fingers."

"That's my good fucking girl." I circle her clit at the same pace as my thrusts. She's so tight, so fucking beautiful laid out for me like this, I need to take my time... even if the clock is working against us.

Untying Ingrid's hands, she slides them to her breasts, tweaking her nipples, as she whispers, "Harder, Cay." There's no way I could ever say no to her, even if it makes me come too quickly. I increase the pressure on her clit and thrust harder, but not faster. "Right there."

I need to get closer.

Angling her legs to the sides a bit, I brace my hand above her head and lean in to kiss her. The sounds of her moans mingle with the slaps of our bodies, and I tug on her bottom lip with my teeth as I pull away. "*Mine.*"

"Always yours." Her whimpered words are my undoing, and with one last thrust, I come deep in her ass.

Ingrid still owes me one more. Remaining inside her, I press two fingers into her pussy and curl them, teasing her until she's writhing beneath me. She grips the nape of my neck and pulls my lips back to hers. It's rough, full of fire, and I can't fucking get enough. Her pussy begins fluttering around my fingers, so I pick up my pace and circle her clit with my thumb. All at once, she clenches, biting my lip hard as she comes. She shuts her eyes, and I take in the sight of the most beautiful woman in the world whimpering in pleasure. The pulsing doesn't subside for at least two minutes, keeping my fingers firmly inside her.

We're both catching our breaths when I hear the front door close, and Cass calling into the house, "Ingrid! I have news! I've met someone. I want to tell you about him before you have to leave for Los Angeles."

"Oh, fuck!" Ingrid yelps, and I carefully slide my cock and fingers out of her. She yells to Cass, "Getting dressed, I'll be out in a second!"

It's too late.

"My eyes!" Cass shields them and turns around. "Why didn't you warn me Cay was home?"

"I said I was getting dressed!"

"I've seen you naked no less than a hundred times. Fuck, I just got dangerously close to seeing my brother's bare ass. Is the honeymoon stage over yet? It's been years!" she harrumphs. "Can you guys get dressed? I need to talk to Ingrid about something."

She storms out, and I kiss Ingrid a final time and quickly get dressed. "Locks... on all the doors."

"Agreed," she laughs. "Can you pick up Darcy from preschool?"

"Of course." I frown. Even after all these years, she forgets we're doing this *together*.

Ingrid swipes her thumb between my brows, relaxing my expression. "I love you, husband." She knows damn well it gets me every time. If Cass wasn't here, I'd show Ingrid just how much I love it when she claims me as hers.

I steal another kiss and speak against her lips, "I love you, too, wife."

# loved never yours?

I hope you loved reading Ingrid and Caleb's story as much as I loved writing it! Cassidy and Travis' story is next in the series, so you'll be able to see more of Ingrid, Caleb, Darcy, Seb and Smitten in *Always Heated!*

Wherever you feel most comfortable, please consider leaving a review on Goodreads, Amazon, or social media! Your honest review means the world to me.

To keep up with all of my upcoming releases, be sure to follow me over on Amazon!

*xoxo,*
*Irene*

# acknowledgments

First, I would like to thank my BFD author besties. You ladies are incredible! I'm so grateful for your friendship and I couldn't have done this without you.

To my beta readers Amanda and Valerie — You are amazing! Thank you for reading this one last minute for me!

To my editor Katie — Thank you for tolerating this ridiculous book. I know it's different from my funny smut, so I appreciate you taking on this one! Do we keep this emotional damage going, or…?

To my proofreader Kendra — You are the sunshine and the moon, all wrapped into one! Thank you for being my final touch on this project.

To my readers — I'm sorry. I know you thought I was kidding when I said this was unlike any other book I've written. Do you believe me now?

Finally, thank you to all of my author friends for not letting my imposter syndrome take over, my "real life" friends for believing in me, and my family for putting up with my silly little dream of becoming a published author.

# about irene

Irene Bahrd is a feisty Capricorn and one of the most avid readers you will ever meet. Her favorite genres to read or write include romantic comedies, political romance, romantasy, and the occasional contemporary or dark romance.

She started her writing journey as a dare from a friend, after recounting dating stories from her early twenties. They inspired her to write spicy romantic comedies and parodies that feature a variety of book boyfriends—though most are cinnamon roll golden retrievers. Many of her stories contain LGBTQIA+, disabled, and neurodivergent characters.

Irene can be found on Instagram and TikTok under @irenebahrdauthor

# also by irene bahrd

Arranged Vacancy

Absolute Majority

Accepted Precedent

## Stand Alone ErotiComs

Flexible Standards

Royally Cuffed

Hard to Swallow

## Holiday ErotiCom Novella Series

Merry in Spite

ForNever Mine

Summer of the Switch

Haunted Happenstance

Save a Horse

## Expect the Unexpected Parody Novella Duet

Undeclared Heir

Undecided Heiress

## Pelligini Crime Daddies Parody Novella Duet

Running from the Garden with Eden

Not My Bodyguard's Keeper

## Magical Mischief Parody Novella Series

Unshifted

Uncharmed

## Thirst Trap Book Boyfriends Satire Series

Trapp Temptations: Vol. 1

Trapp Temptations: Vol. 2

Printed in Great Britain
by Amazon